For my grandson,
Beckett, with love

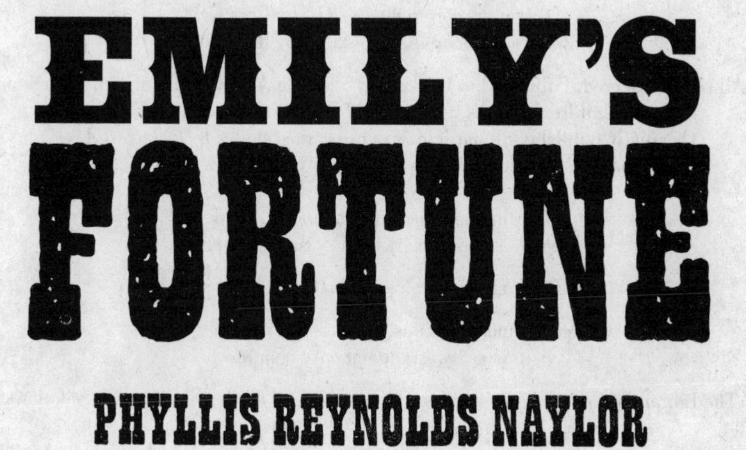

ILLUSTRATED BY ROSS COLLINS

A YEARLING BOOK

 Published in the United States by Yearling, an imprint of Random House Children's Books, a division of Random House, Inc., New York.
Originally published in hardcover in the United States by Delacorte Press, an imprint of Random House Children's Books, New York, in 2010.

Yearling and the jumping horse design are registered trademarks of Random House, Inc.

Visit us on the Web! www.randomhouse.com/kids

Educators and librarians, for a variety of teaching tools, visit us at www.randomhouse.com/teachers

The Library of Congress has cataloged the hardcover edition of this work as follows:
Naylor, Phyllis Reynolds.
Emily's fortune / Phyllis Reynolds Naylor.—1st ed.
p. cm.
Summary: While traveling to her aunt's home in Redbud by train and stagecoach, quiet young Emily and her turtle, Rufus, team up with Jackson, fellow orphan and troublemaker extraordinaire, to outsmart mean Uncle Victor, who is after Emily's inheritance.
ISBN 978-0-385-73616-9 (trade)—ISBN 978-0-385-90589-3 (lib. bdg.)—
ISBN 978-0-375-89650-7 (ebook)
[1. Orphans—Fiction. 2. Voyages and travels—Fiction. 3. Inheritance and succession—Fiction. 4. Uncles—Fiction. 5. West (U.S.)—History—19th century—Fiction.] I. Title.
PZ7.N24Em 2010
[Fic]—dc22
200901396

ISBN 978-0-375-84492-8 (pbk.)

Printed in the United States of America
10 9 8 7 6 5 4

First Yearling Edition 2011

Random House Children's Books supports the First Amendment and celebrates the right to read.

CONTENTS

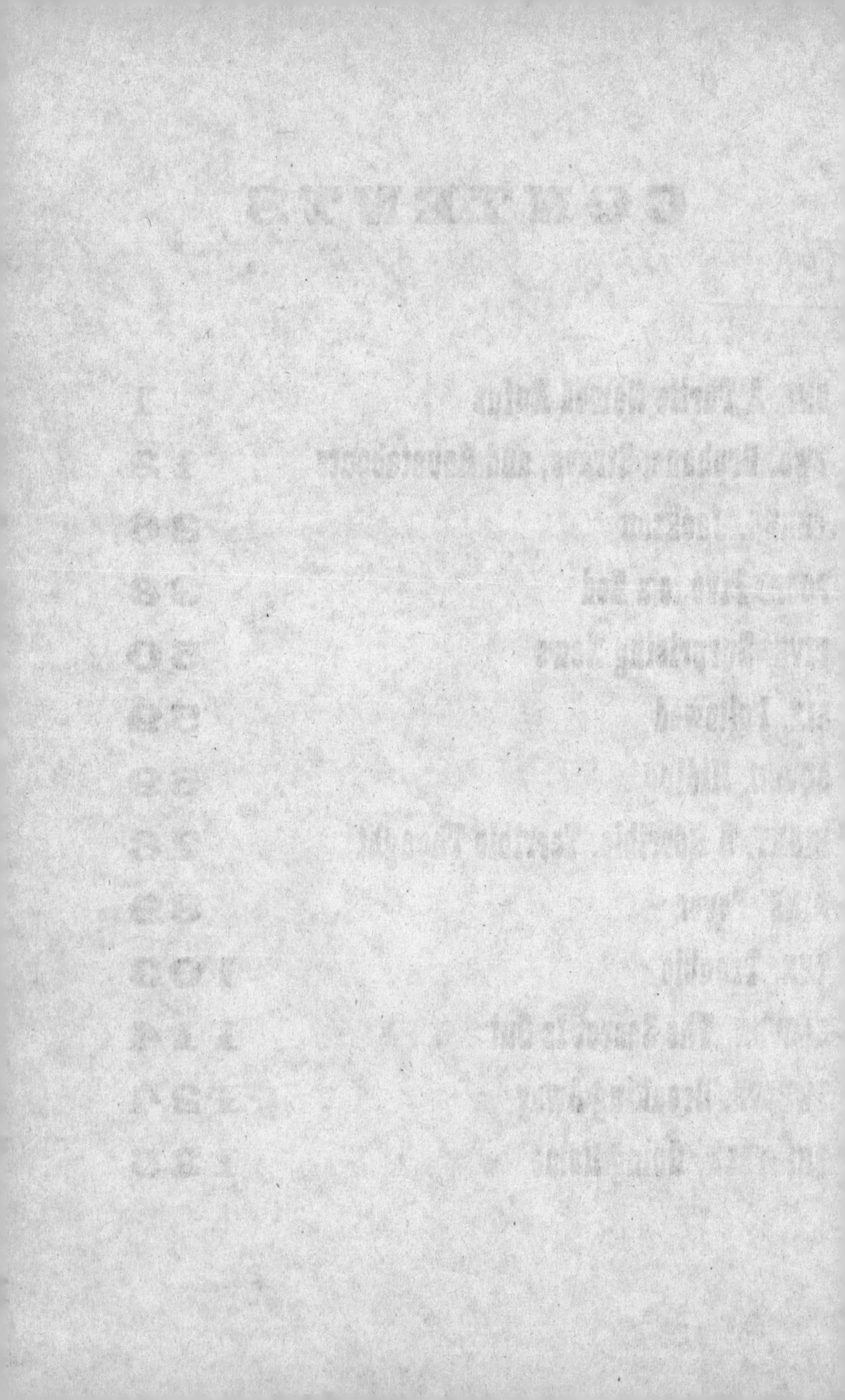

ONE
A Turtle Named Rufus

When eight-year-old Emily found herself alone in the world, she didn't have much: a few dresses, a couple of books, and a small green turtle named Rufus.

She also had her socks and underwear. Emily never said *underwear* aloud—never said *any*thing very loud—because her mother worked for the wealthy Miss Luella Nash, and the old woman liked *quiet.* Peace and quiet. Calm and order. Crackers and cheese, and a perfectly brewed cup of tea.

When she drove her carriage, however—and Luella always insisted on driving herself—she went a little bit crazy. Her neighbors called her Loony Lu. Her eyes would bulge, her mouth would grin, and she would lean so far forward she could have grabbed the horse by its tail.

"Faster!" she would call. "*Faster!*" And she'd slap the reins against the animal's side until the horse went racing through the streets of the town and the carriage rocked from side to side.

"There goes Loony Lu!" people would say.

Once she was home again, however, Miss Luella Nash would hand the reins to a servant, straighten her bonnet, and step elegantly from the carriage, nodding politely to the neighbors who studied her from beyond the gate.

As for little Emily, her father had died in a steamboat accident when she was just a baby. Ever since, she and her mother had lived in Luella's big house, in the back room behind the kitchen.

Sometimes Emily's mother took her into the parlor to visit Miss Nash. Emily had to make sure that her hair was curled, her ears were clean, her nose was blown, her teeth were brushed, her nails were trimmed, her clothes were pressed, and her socks had not a wrinkle in them. She even took off her shoes so they wouldn't make any noise. And on the rare occasion that Miss Luella Nash asked her a question, Emily answered in a voice so soft it could have been the squeak of the lid on a mustard jar.

Miss Luella Nash seemed to believe that grown-ups were always right. If the carriage master upset the horses and said that the gardener had done it, Luella Nash believed him. If the gardener bumped the rose trellis and said that the maid had done it, Luella Nash believed him too. And if the maid knocked over a vase and said that Emily had done it, then of course Luella Nash believed that also.

"Dismissed!" she would say to Emily at the end of a visit, waving the fingers of one hand and sending her from the room.

So little Emily was not allowed to be seen or heard unless she was on her best behavior, and Miss Nash would not let her do any work about the place, except for buttoning her own dresses and tying her own shoes, combing her own hair and brushing her own teeth. Emily was not allowed to help the servants with the dusting because Miss Nash wanted it done just so. She could not feed the chickens, wash the dishes, husk the corn, gather the berries, or mop the floor. Everything had to be done exactly as Luella Nash thought right.

Emily's mother encouraged her to do as much as

possible in the room they shared. Emily learned to make a bed and shake a rug and sweep a floor and scrub a tub. But most of the time she could only sit at the window and watch the neighbor children at play. She was not allowed to join them because she might get hurt, Miss Nash had said. She was not allowed to go to school because she might learn bad words. Her mother taught her to read and write, but still . . . *How will I ever get along in the world if I can't* do *anything?* Emily asked Rufus, her turtle, as he sat on the back of her hand and together they watched the world beyond the window.

•••

One terrible day, however, something awful happened: Constance, Emily's mother, had gone to market with Miss Nash, and on their way home, with Luella at the reins, the carriage tipped over and fell into the river. Only the horse was saved.

Emily was now an orphan.

"What will become of me?" she cried. "Where will I go?" Her sobs were no louder than the little *puff-puff-puff*s she used to make blowing soap bubbles on the porch with her mother.

The neighbors—Mrs. Ready, Mrs. Aim, and Mrs. Fire—tried to help.

Mrs. Ready always repeated the problem.

Mrs. Aim always asked the question.

And Mrs. Fire always had an answer.

"She doesn't know what will happen to her," said Mrs. Ready.

"Did Constance have a plan?" asked Mrs. Aim.

"We will ask Emily and see," said Mrs. Fire. So they did.

Emily wiped her eyes with one small fist. "Mother said that if anything ever happened to her, I should go live with the one who loved me most," she whispered, weeping.

"And who would that be?" the women wanted to know.

"I have an aunt Hilda in Redbud," Emily breathed.

"What?" the women said, leaning forward so they could hear. "An anthill in Bedbug?"

"Aunt Hilda in Redbud," Emily repeated, a bit louder. "She is my aunt by marriage."

"An aunt by marriage in Redbud," Mrs. Ready echoed.

But Mrs. Aim asked the question: "Don't you have any blood relatives?"

"Only Uncle Victor," Emily whispered, more softly than ever.

"What?" asked Mrs. Aim, leaning closer still. "Old hunk of pickle?"

"Only Uncle Victor," Emily replied, "but please don't send me to live with him. I don't even know where he is."

Emily didn't want to talk about her uncle Victor, on her mother's side of the family, because she did not want to live with him. She was sure he didn't love her at all. It was true she had only met Aunt Hilda, her father's sister-in-law, once. But she remembered a kind face, a warm lap, and big arms that hugged her tight. Aunt Hilda also sent cookies at Christmas.

Uncle Victor, however, had the silver-black hair of a wolf, the eyes of a weasel, the growl of a bear, and a tiger tattoo on his arm. He had a gold tooth that gleamed when he opened his mouth, and he could crack two walnuts in the palm of one hand just by squeezing his fist. He never came to see Emily's mother unless he wanted money. The only thing Uncle Victor was afraid of, it seemed, was love.

"Why don't you like him, child?" the women questioned.

"He's never said a kind word to me or my mother," replied Emily. "The last time he visited us, when I was six, he took our money and made my mother cry."

"Why, we've seen him here ourselves," said Mrs. Ready, remembering.

"And he is your mother's brother?" asked Mrs. Aim. "How awful!"

"Then we shall write to your aunt Hilda and ask if she will take you in," said Mrs. Fire, and off the letter went.

• • •

Meanwhile, the servants began to close up Miss Luella Nash's house. They polished the silver and put it away. They aired out the blankets and put them in chests. They covered the chairs and lowered the blinds. Emily was afraid they might pack her up too, so she was even quieter than usual. She sat on the back steps with Rufus and stroked his tiny head with one finger.

Lawyers came in and out, studying the paintings on the walls and writing numbers in their books. They argued over the lamps, counted the candlesticks, and bumped into each other in the hallways.

Finally a letter arrived from Aunt Hilda:

> My dear Emily,
>
> What sad news it is about your mother. Of course you may come and live with me. I have a small house here in Redbud, and I love to cook. Like your mother, I don't have much money, but I raise chickens and a few sheep, and there are wide-open spaces where you can play. My cat and dog will keep us company.
>
> I'll be watching for you every time a stagecoach comes in.
>
> Your loving
> Aunt Hilda

"How will I get to Redbud?" asked Emily.

It was a long way off, the neighbors explained, and the journey would take many days. They would drive her to the train station themselves, and once she got to Trumpet Junction, a stagecoach would take her the rest of the way.

"I wonder if Emily can do this," said Mrs. Ready anxiously. "She has never done much of anything before."

Mrs. Aim looked at Emily. "Can you do this, child?" she asked. "Can you stand the stopping and starting, the thumping and bumping, the swinging and swaying, and the smell of four sweaty horses?"

"I *must,*" Emily whispered determinedly.

"And she *will!*" said Mrs. Fire. "A train leaves for Trumpet Junction this very day, so let's pack her things in a carpetbag and get her to the station."

But somebody else was on the way

to Luella's big house!

Now, who in flippin' flapjacks could it be?

TWO
Orphans, Strays, and Roustabouts

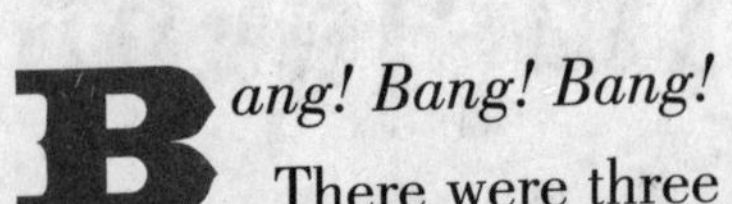

Bang! Bang! Bang!

There were three heavy knocks on the door of Luella Nash's big white house. With all the servants busy upstairs and the neighbor women at work in the kitchen, it was Emily who answered.

There stood a large woman in a gray dress, gray shoes, and a gray hat over her gray hair. She was holding a gray notebook in her hands.

"Emily Wiggins?" the woman asked. "The child who never goes to school?"

Emily swallowed. "Yes," she said, in her teeny, tiny voice.

"I am Miss Catchum," the woman said. "Your present circumstances have been brought to our attention. It is my job to find a place for you to live, now that your dear departed mother is gone." She dabbed at her eye with a handkerchief, but Emily didn't see any trace of a tear.

"But I *have* a place to live," Emily told her quickly. "I have an aunt Hilda down in Redbud."

"I know, but she is only your aunt by marriage," Miss Catchum said. "I have looked up your records and I see that your closest living blood relative is your mother's brother, Victor. According to clause number thirty-one D in paragraph ninety-two of section one hundred and eight of the Regulations Regarding Orphaned Children, such children are to be kept off the streets at all costs by residing with their closest living relative, their next of kin."

Thumpa thumpa thumpa, went Emily's heart.

"But . . . he won't want me!" she protested. "He doesn't even like me! He doesn't like children at all!"

"How do you know unless we ask him?" said Miss Catchum. "Our office gets a bonus for every child we place with a relative, and a super-duper-dinger-zinger bonus if it's the closest living relative of the

mother herself. I'm sure your uncle Victor will look deep in his heart and provide for his orphaned niece."

Emily was not so sure. The man with the silver-black hair of a wolf and the eyes of a weasel and the growl of a bear and the tiger tattoo had never sat Emily on his lap, never given her a hug, and *certainly* never sent cookies at Christmas. Emily knew without a doubt that if Uncle Victor looked deep in his heart, he would only see a way to get rid of her.

Mrs. Ready, Mrs. Aim, and Mrs. Fire had been listening from the hallway, and together they came to the door.

"Please let Emily live with one of us until the matter can be settled," said Mrs. Fire. "We shall take the best care of her."

"I'm afraid that wouldn't do," said Miss Catchum. "She might get away, and then I would lose my super-duper-dinger-zinger bonus. The orphans' home will lock her in until her uncle can be found." She turned once more to Emily. "Get your things together, dearie, and I'll be back around shortly to pick you up." The woman in the gray dress and hat and shoes went out to her gray carriage with her gray notebook and shook the reins of her horse. A gray one.

As soon as she had gone, the neighbor women put their heads together.

"Now, that's a problem," said Mrs. Ready.

"How can they send her to live with someone who doesn't even like children?" asked Mrs. Aim.

"They shouldn't and they *won't*!" Mrs. Fire declared. "We must see that Emily is on that train before Miss Catchum comes to collect her."

And before Emily could say "Ready . . . Aim . . . Fire," the women finished packing her carpetbag, then hustled her and the little box that held Rufus out to their carriage next door.

Halfway to the train station, they saw a carriage coming toward them. A sign on the driver's door read:

CATCHUM CHILD-CATCHING SERVICES
ORPHANS, STRAYS, AND ROUSTABOUTS
ROUNDED UP QUICKLY

Mrs. Ready and Mrs. Aim pushed Emily to the floor, where she couldn't be seen, and Mrs. Fire kept her eyes straight ahead as they passed the Catchum carriage. When the danger was gone, Emily crawled back up on the seat, her bonnet dangling from one ear, and the horse galloped on.

When they reached the station, the kind women bought a ticket for Emily and gave her the lunch they had prepared. Then they took her out to the track, where the big black engine was belching smoke and shooting sparks.

"Remember, dear Emily, that you are a little child traveling alone," said Mrs. Ready.

"And what should such a child do?" asked Mrs. Aim.

"She should keep her eyes open, her ears clean, and her chin up," said Mrs. Fire.

"And be prepared for anything," the three women said together.

Emily thanked them for their help and climbed aboard. The whistle blew, the engine belched again, and the cars jerked forward. It was all Emily could do to remain upright.

• • •

She found a seat by a window and set the carpetbag at her feet. It was very crowded in the car and the benches were hard, with wooden backs. Emily pressed her face to the glass and waved to the three women who had been so helpful.

Far off in the distance she could see a tiny white speck up on a hill. She knew it was the last she would see of the big white house where she had lived since she was a baby.

Puff, puff, puff, went the steam engine. *Wheet, wheet, wheet,* went the whistle.

Emily thought she might fall asleep to the rhythm, but suddenly a gray horse pulling a gray carriage came dashing along the platform. Emily looked over to see Miss Catchum leaning out her window yelling, "Stop! Stop!" and waving a handful of papers.

Emily gripped the edge of her seat with her fingers. But the big iron wheels of the train were going faster, and before long Miss Catchum, the station, and the three neighbor women were far behind. Emily sat back and let out a long breath.

When her heartbeat had slowed to normal, she took Rufus out of his box with the small holes in the lid. She let him crawl along her arm so that he could see out the window too. She had no father, no mother now, and no home till she got to Aunt Hilda's. All she had was a little green turtle, some lunch, and a carpetbag of clothes. A tear rolled down her cheek and fell on the turtle's face. Rufus tipped back his head and drank it.

Then Emily remembered something else about Uncle Victor. The last time he had come to visit, two years before, he had made her mother cry, as usual, and Emily had glared at him from the doorway.

"Whatcha got there?" he'd growled, his weasel-like eyes looking at Emily's cupped hands. "Something for me?"

"No," Emily had told him. "It's Rufus, my new turtle. Mother bought him for me."

"Ha!" said Uncle Victor, and his "Ha!" sounded

like gravel hitting the side of a barn. "All a turtle's good for is turtle soup."

Emily had run and hidden in a closet. And after Uncle Victor left the house that day with some of Mother's money, Emily had hoped he would never come back. Now, of course, there was nothing for him to come back *for.*

After Rufus had crawled around a bit, Emily gently put him back in his box. "You are all I have in this world, and I'll take care of you forever," she promised.

Except for church on Sundays, Emily had never been with so many people all crowded together. Was everyone in the world going to Trumpet Junction? she wondered, looking at the dozens of bags and boxes tucked beneath the seats.

The man beside Emily was falling asleep. His head tipped back and his mouth fell open. *Sssnnnoooggghhh,* he went.

The woman next to him was knitting a cap. *Click, click, click,* went her needles.

The small child at the end of the row was wailing

loudly, *Wah, wah, wah,* and wiping her eyes with one smudgy fist.

Row after row of people filled the train car, and a potbellied stove in the middle kept some passengers too hot, while those around the edges of the car were too cold.

Every so often the train jerked, or rocked from side to side. If it rocked to the left, Emily tipped against the sleeping man. If it tipped to the right, the sleeping man leaned over on Emily and almost flattened her against the window.

After several hours, the small child who had been wailing wanted to see out the window, and Emily kindly agreed to change places. Now the mother and child sat by the window, and Emily sat at the end of the bench on the aisle. And next time, when the car tipped, everyone toppled over onto Emily, and Emily landed on the floor.

• • •

Once, when Emily opened the lid of Rufus's box and let him crawl around her lap, a short woman across the aisle looked at her in disgust.

"Throw that slimy creature away, child!" she scolded. "Did your mother teach you no manners?"

"My . . . my mother gave him to me," Emily tried to explain, but the short woman shook her head.

"Don't lie," she told her, and Emily put Rufus back in his box. It was no surprise to her that many grown-ups didn't listen.

As the hours went on, the air grew stale and smelly. Some people were eating supper. Some of the men were smoking cigars. At different stops, vendors would hop aboard and race up and down the aisles, selling soap or soup or bread before the train moved on again.

Emily had no money to buy food, but she did have the lunch bag the neighbors had given her. She opened it up and found a feast: a piece of cold chicken, a sausage, a round of cheese, a half loaf of bread, some carrots, an orange, and a thick slice of caramel cake. She ate the chicken but saved the rest, and gave Rufus a tiny bite of carrot.

As darkness fell, the conductor lit the oil lamps so that passengers could see their way to the foul toilet in a closet at the end of the car. Emily held her breath when she used the closet. She couldn't imagine wealthy Miss Nash, who had liked things clean and tidy, ever using such a dirty closet at all.

When it was time to sleep, Emily wondered if she possibly could. But she placed her carpetbag on her lap as a pillow, laid her head on it, wrapped her arms around it, and fell into a deep slumber.

The next morning she was awakened by the conductor calling, "This is as far as the train goes, folks! All out for Trumpet Junction."

The weary passengers picked up their squabbling children, their bawling babies, their boxes and bags and coats and bonnets, and started for the door.

Emily got off the train with the others, but she wasn't sure where to go next.

Wagons were rattling back and forth in front of the train station. Horses and riders, carts and bicycles.

She was following the crowd to a building with a sign that read OVERHILL STAGECOACH COMPANY when suddenly her heart began to pound, her hands began to sweat, and her knees began to tremble, for a carriage was rolling right toward her.

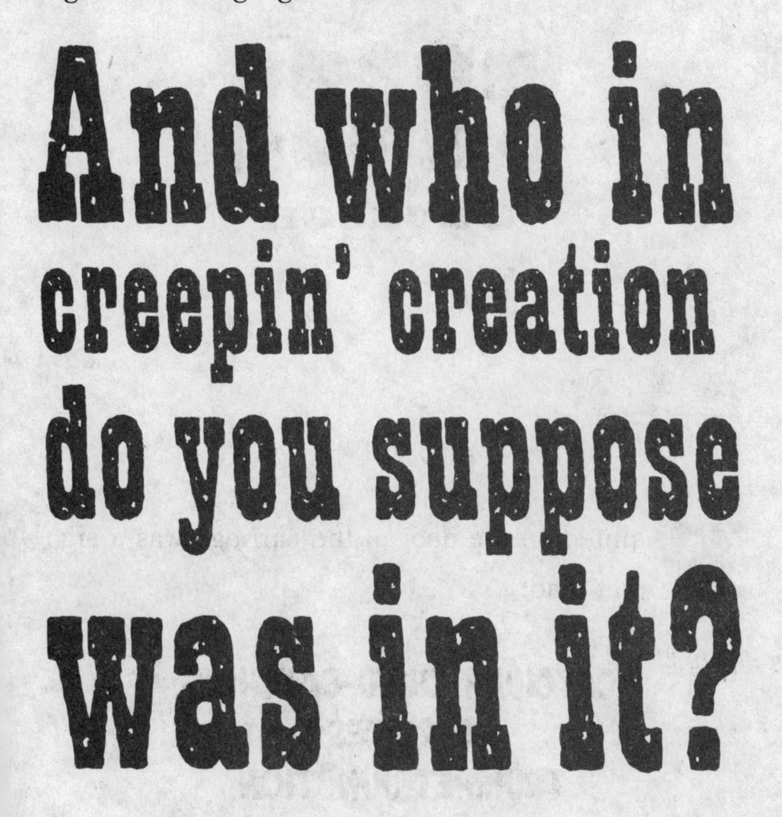

THREE

Jackson

Painted on the door of the carriage was a sign that read:

CATCHUM CHILD-CATCHING
SERVICES
TRUMPET JUNCTION
BRANCH
ORPHANS, STRAYS, AND
ROUSTABOUTS
ROUNDED UP QUICKLY

Emily jumped behind a mail cart so fast that she bumped into a boy in a faded brown jacket.

"Hey!" he said. "Watch where you're going!" And then, "You're an orphan too, aren't you?"

Emily could hardly see the boy's eyes because he wore a flat round cap that stuck out over his forehead. But she noticed that he had freckles like hers and the same color of brown hair sticking out from under his cap. And though he appeared to be a year or two older than she was, he wasn't that much larger.

But how *rude* he was! And how did he know she was an orphan? She stared down at her clothes, almost expecting to see the letters *o-r-p-h-a-n* on each of her high-topped shoes.

"How did you *know*?" she asked him.

He shrugged. "Saw you trying to hide from the Child Catchers, just like I used to do."

"Where are you going?" she asked.

"Who knows?" answered the boy. "Got me a ticket to some family out west, but they probably won't like me any more'n the last family did.

Child Catchers will send you anywhere if they can make a buck. I'm Jackson," he told her.

"I'm Emily," she said.

"What you got in your bag?" Jackson asked.

Emily noticed that Jackson had only a small parcel tucked under his arm and was wearing shoes that looked a little too big.

"Just . . . clothes," she answered, and added, "I don't have any money," in case he was going to ask.

Jackson pointed toward the door of Overhill Stagecoach Company. "They told us if we go in there, they'll give us something to eat before we get on board," he said.

So Emily followed him inside, where a large map on the wall showed the stops the stagecoach would make between Trumpet Junction and Redbud, and the stops beyond that, all the way to the ocean. It would take five days and five nights just to get to Redbud, according to the man who was checking tickets. That was a long time to be bumping along on your bottom, Emily thought.

A woman behind a table was ladling soup into tin cups and offering them with crackers to all the passengers. Emily was surprised to see that there were no spoons, so she sipped her soup daintily. But Jackson greedily gulped his down, then gave a loud belch.

Beside the map on the wall, there was a large sign:

Hints for Travelers

1. Don't complain about the food.
2. Don't smoke a strong pipe.
3. Don't lop over on your neighbor when sleeping.
4. Don't spit on the floor.
5. Wash your feet before starting the trip.

Emily had taken a bath the night before she'd gotten on the train, but she was quite sure that some of the other passengers had not. Jackson, in fact, looked as though he hadn't washed his face for a week.

"So what happened to your ma?" he asked her.

"She died in a carriage accident," Emily said, and tears came to her eyes, just remembering.

"What about your pa?"

"He died when a steamboat sank," Emily told him.

"What you got in that box?" asked Jackson.

Emily opened the lid and showed him her turtle. "His name is Rufus, and he's my best friend in the whole world," she said.

Jackson gave a snort, but Emily let him hold the turtle for a minute anyway. And she noticed that when he returned Rufus to the box, he did it gently.

Then he went to the door and looked around. "The Child Catchers are gone," he said. "Want to go outside and see the horses?" Emily picked up her bag, Jackson picked up his parcel, and out they went.

The Overhill stagecoach was bigger than any Emily had ever seen. It was bright red. The four horses with yellow harnesses pawed at the ground, eager to be off.

A man with a whip came out of the building and Emily shrank back in fear. Then she realized that he was the driver, dressed in a dark blue jacket with gold buttons.

"Stagecoach to the West!" he called. "Gather here!"

Emily could not believe the number of people who

moved forward. She could not believe all they carried. A box poked her in the back. A basket bopped her on the head. She had thought that perhaps four people could fit inside, and after three women and two men got aboard, then Jackson, who pushed on ahead, she was afraid there would be no room for her. Yet two more men got on, and finally the driver picked her up with her bag and squeezed her onto a seat.

Three people sat on the backseat, facing forward. Three people sat on the middle seat, and three people sat on the front seat, facing backward. Bags and boxes were crammed under seats and on laps. Emily kept her lunch sack and carpetbag on her lap so she could take out Rufus's box and let him have a bit of air.

When everyone was settled at last, the coachman sprang up to the driver's box outside. After a blast of his bugle and a crack of the driver's whip, the stage-coach lurched forward with a creak and squeak, and headed west.

• • •

Emily had been looking forward to seeing new places, but she soon discovered how tiresome it was sitting in the same position for hours at a time. When the windows were up, it was too warm. When the windows were down, dust blew in, filling her nose and making her sneeze.

She was sitting in the front row, with Jackson facing her. His cap was tipped backward now, and she could see that his eyes were green like her own. But every time he caught her looking at him, he made a face.

Then he started the copycat game. If Emily crossed her arms over her chest, Jackson crossed his arms. If Emily sighed, Jackson sighed. If she ignored him completely, he slid down in his seat until his bony knees were bumping hers, and kicked her shoes with his feet.

Please stop it, Emily mouthed at him.

Please stop it, Jackson mouthed back.

Were all boys this rude? she asked herself. No wonder Luella Nash hadn't wanted her to go to school with the other children.

The coach stopped every fifteen miles or so for a fresh team of horses. Sometimes the driver let the passengers get out and stretch a bit. Other times, a new team was harnessed and ready, and the coach wheels hardly stopped rolling before they were off again.

Finally, a blast of the driver's bugle announced their arrival at Callaway's Inn, where all the passengers were given a meal. It was a busy place, and even the porch was crowded. Some people sat on benches, others sat in rockers, and still more stood reading the daily newspapers that had been tacked up on the porch wall.

Inside the inn, Emily was almost too tired to chew. But she knew she ought to eat when she was given food, so that she could save what was in her lunch sack for later. She ate until she was full, and Jackson reached over to take what she'd left on her plate.

When it was time to get on board again, the driver came up to the table where Emily and Jackson were sitting.

"We have a problem," he told them. "There's a lady and her husband whose daughter out west is very sick. They need to get there as soon as possible, so we're asking if you'll give up your places in the coach. We'll make sure you get on the next one."

"Yeah, and when will that be?" asked Jackson.

"Another will be along in two days, and the innkeeper says you may stay here until it comes," the driver said. "The Overhill Stagecoach Company will pay for your room and board."

Emily did not want to keep the man and woman from seeing their sick daughter. She knew that Aunt Hilda did not expect her at any particular time, and

that if she did not arrive on a stagecoach one day, she would arrive another. She would willingly give up her seat if only they would take Jackson. She did not want to have to stare at him and his silly faces all the way to Redbud. But no, two seats were needed, not one.

"This is certainly a fine pickle of a problem," Mrs. Ready would say.

"Should she go or should she stay?" Mrs. Aim would ask.

And Emily could almost hear Mrs. Fire give the answer: "She should stay so that the couple can see their sick daughter, and she should tell that Jackson boy to mind his own business."

"I'll give up my seat if I can ride the next stage-coach," Emily said at last.

Jackson only shrugged. "She stays, I stay," he said.

So Emily and Jackson could only watch as the other passengers climbed back in, along with the man and woman whose daughter was sick.

The bugle blew, the whip cracked, and with creaks and squeaks, off went the coach, leaving Emily and Jackson looking after it. But with all the people who were crowding the porch, as well as the rooms inside,

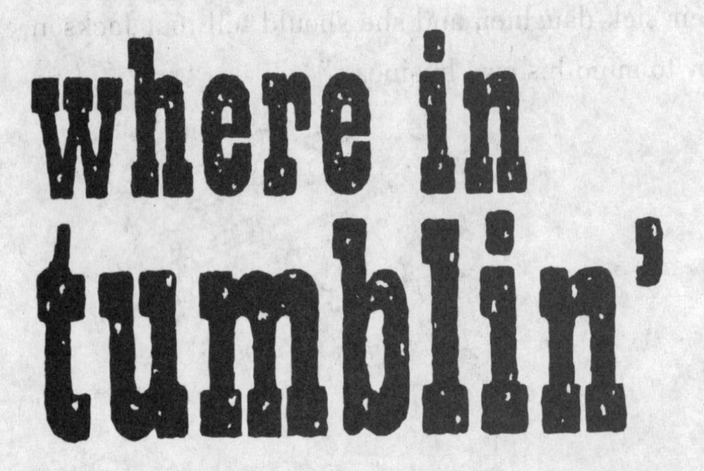

tarnation was Emily supposed to sleep?

FOUR
Five to a Bed

If she had to spend the next two days with someone, Emily thought, why couldn't it be a quiet girl with a book under her arm?

But Jackson motioned for her to follow him.

"Come on!" he said. "Let's look around."

She might as well, Emily thought, because the inn was full of people—peddlers wanting a mug of tea, visitors needing a place to sleep. Little groups of travelers stood around on the porch reading the newspapers, and families milled about in the front yard, letting their children tumble and yell before they started off again on their journeys.

Emily put her lunch sack and Rufus's box in her carpetbag, then grabbed its wooden handles and followed Jackson around the inn. There were other buildings out back—a springhouse, a carriage house, a stable, a barn.

She peeked inside the springhouse when Jackson opened the creaky door. It was just a small hut built over a spring. Crocks of butter and eggs cooled in the trickling water.

Jackson grinned as he closed the door again. "When everyone's asleep tonight, we could take those eggs and smash 'em on the porch," he said.

Emily stared at him. "What for?" she asked.

Jackson shrugged. "I dunno. Something to do," he told her.

They walked over to the carriage house, where two small buggies sat, whips across the seats.

"We could hide those whips in the bushes," Jackson said. "They'd have to hunt all day to find 'em."

"Why would you want to do *that*?" Emily asked.

"Cause a little excitement, maybe," said Jackson.

And when they poked their heads into the stable, Jackson talked about letting the horses out. *No wonder the last family Jackson stayed with didn't want him,* Emily thought.

"Are you always looking for trouble?" she asked as they wandered along the fence beside the pasture.

"Not always," said Jackson.

"Then what else do you like to do?"

"I like to climb trees. I like to chase rabbits. I like to wade in creeks and catch crawdads."

"I've never climbed a tree in my life," said Emily.

Jackson studied her for a moment. "Your arms are too short; legs are too weak," he said.

"They are not!" said Emily.

"Ha! You couldn't climb a tree if the devil was after you," he jeered.

What made this dirty-faced boy so awful? Emily wondered. There was a tree up ahead, and Emily marched over. "I could too!" she declared, but when they got there, her heart pounding, she said, "Boys first." Then she added, uncertainly, "It's the polite thing to do."

"Well, I've never been polite in my life," said Jackson, "but I'll show you how to climb a tree."

Holding on to a post, the skinny boy hoisted himself to the top of the wood-and-wire fence, then braced one hand against the tree and stood up on the top rail. He reached both hands toward the lowest branch, grabbed it, then in one swift move swung a leg over it and pulled himself up to a sitting position.

Once again, he stood, reached for the next branch, threw a leg over, and climbed up.

"Your turn!" he called.

Emily set her bag on the ground. Her throat felt dry and her hands were sweaty. She held on to the post, and though her feet slipped and slid against the wire, she finally managed to get onto the top rail. But when she tried to stand up on it, she felt herself being yanked backward, and sat down with a bump.

Jackson cackled gleefully in the branches above.

Emily tried again, but once more she felt herself being yanked backward onto the wooden rail.

"Haw haw!" came Jackson's voice above her. "It's your dress! It's snagged on the wire."

Emily looked down and unhooked the hem of her dress. But when she freed herself at last and shakily stood up, the first branch of the maple tree was just beyond her reach. Bracing one hand against the tree trunk, she stood on tiptoe and stretched her other arm as high as she could, but her fingertips barely touched the branch.

"Hee hee ha ha!" chortled Jackson, and this made Emily angry indeed. This time she stretched her arms as high as they would go and gave a little jump. The next thing she knew, she was hanging on to the branch, her feet swinging back and forth in the air.

"J-J-Jackson!" she called shakily. "Help me!"

He peered down at her. "Well," he said, "I could stomp on your fingers. . . ."

"Jackson!" she pleaded.

"Swing your legs over to the tree trunk and walk yourself up to the branch. Then flop one leg over," he told her.

Emily's feet flailed back and forth until they found the trunk, scraping and skidding against the bark.

One of her shoes fell off, and Jackson howled some more. But finally, holding the branch with both hands, she walked her feet up the trunk to the branch where she clung, and threw one leg over, finally getting on top of it.

"Well," Jackson said. "You made it this far, but you can't say you've climbed a tree until you go one branch more."

Emily didn't want to hear it. She was too frightened to go up and too frightened to go down. She imagined that she would spend the rest of her life wrapped around that branch.

But at last she gained the courage to sit up, and she found that the next branch was closer than she had thought. And with a little help from Jackson, she managed to get up onto the limb beside him. Shakily she sat up and looked about.

"I've never been this high before," she confided. "Not even on a stepladder."

"Ha!" said Jackson. "I've hid in a tree so many times I'm about to grow leaves. Every time somebody wants to beat me, I'm up a tree."

"Oh, lordy, whatever happened to your parents?" Emily asked.

"My ma ran off, and Pa got sick and died," Jackson told her. "I'm a bad-luck kid for sure."

What would Luella Nash say about her sitting in a tree beside a boy who was always in trouble? Emily wondered. It didn't matter much, since she liked being up this high, where she could see carriages far out on the road, and a creek running along the edge of a wood.

Suddenly Jackson slid off the branch onto the limb below.

"C'mon," he said. "They're lighting the lanterns on the porch and folks'll be going to bed. If you don't find a place early, you'll end up on the floor."

Emily peered down at the ground beneath them. It seemed a lot scarier going down than it had coming up. "I . . . I can't!" she said, her voice shaky.

"Well, if you don't, you'll sleep in the tree all night," Jackson told her. "Grab hold of the branch you're sitting on and slide your foot down to the next one."

Somehow Emily made it to the limb below, but the fence was too far for her feet to reach. She hung by her hands, feet kicking, and finally she simply let go and fell to the ground with a thump.

For a moment she lay on her back, eyes closed, but when she opened them, she saw a huge hairy face looking down at her with two terrible eyes, and before she could roll away, a huge brown tongue suddenly poked out and licked her face.

Emily screamed, but on the other side of the fence, Jackson was rolling on the ground with laughter, and the big brown cow that had stopped by ambled on to another part of the pasture.

Jackson continued to laugh as Emily climbed back over the fence and found her shoe. He went on hee-hawing as she tied the lace and picked up her carpetbag. But as they walked back to the inn, he said, "Now, listen here, if you don't get a bed, the best place to sleep is under a table, 'cause no one can stumble over you during the night."

No bed? Emily wondered. Things were going from bad to worse. And who would want to give a bed to a dirty girl in a torn dress and wrinkled socks?

Inside, the innkeeper was giving instructions: "Women and girls sleep up," he said, pointing toward the stairs; "men and boys sleep down. Don't sleep with your boots on, don't hog the covers, and no more'n five to a bed."

Emily followed the women and girls, already missing the soft bed she had shared with her mother back in Miss Nash's big house.

There were four bedrooms upstairs, with two beds each. Women were busy setting their bags down, and Emily knew she had to hurry if she wanted any space at all.

Taking off her shoes and socks, she lifted her dress over her head and placed it on a chair. Then she slipped under the covers on one of the beds, and was soon joined by two women on one side of her, one woman on the other.

There were only two pillows, and Emily didn't even get to share one. Her small head sank down between them, where she couldn't see out. When the women on either side of her moved, Emily got an elbow in the ribs, a knee against her leg, an arm across her face. And then the women began to snore.

Sssnnnooog, went the first woman.

Sssnnnooop, went the second.

Sssnnnoooz, went the third.

Bong, bong, bong, went the grandfather clock at the bottom of the stairs.

When the clock struck one in the morning, Emily heard it.

When it struck two, she was still awake. She slept some after that, but at five, when the woman beside her got up to use the chamber pot, Emily saw her chance and slid out of bed. She put on her dress and felt around for her shoes and socks. Then, picking up her carpetbag with Rufus and his little box inside, she made her way downstairs to see if she could find a sofa or chair where she might curl up and sleep a few more hours before breakfast.

But the snoring downstairs was even louder than the snoring up. In the early-morning light, Emily could see men and boys sleeping every which way. There were men under tables, men propped up in chairs. Every sofa had a man on it, and one little boy had rolled himself up in a rug.

There was a faint noise in the kitchen, and Emily wondered if the innkeeper's wife might be up starting breakfast. She tiptoed through the hallway toward the kitchen. She could just make out a sign above the door that read:

CUSTOMERS ARE NOT ALLOWED IN THE KITCHEN.
KEEP OUT!

But all she wanted was a peek.

And what in blinkin' bloomers do you think she saw?

FIVE
Surprising News

There was Jackson by the big iron stove, his hand deep inside the cracker barrel.

"Jackson, what are you *doing*?" Emily whispered. "Didn't you read the sign?"

"What sign?" asked Jackson.

Emily pointed to the door behind her. "Back there. Customers aren't allowed in the kitchen."

"I was hungry," said Jackson, and Emily noticed for the first time just how very thin and bony his face was.

"Well, we shouldn't be here," Emily told him, and

was sure of it when she heard footsteps upstairs. With her carpetbag in one hand, she pulled Jackson out the back door, but not before he had crammed his pockets full of crackers.

"Didn't you get enough to eat last night?" she asked.

"I never get enough to eat," said Jackson. "All they put on my plate was the last ladle of beans. The last bit of bread. A little dried-up piece of meat."

"Well, then," said Emily, opening her carpetbag and pulling out the lunch sack she had been saving. "Let's go eat in the barn."

A small shaft of early-morning light came from a high window inside the barn. There was a huge mound of sweet-smelling hay that almost reached the rafters, and a stall on one side where the cow could rest during the night. It had already been milked and let out to pasture. Emily opened the sack the neighbor women had given her and handed the sausage to Jackson.

"Here," she said.

Jackson reached for it hungrily, then stopped. "But it's yours!" he said.

"We'll share," Emily told him.

She took Rufus out of his box and let him crawl about as she and Jackson had their breakfast. They ate the sausage and the bread and cheese, nibbled some carrots, and devoured the caramel cake. Emily fed another tiny bit of carrot to Rufus.

"Ah!" said Jackson, leaning back in the hay, hands on his belly. "That's the first time I've been full since Christmas."

"What happened at Christmas?" asked Emily.

"I was in an orphanage, and the church ladies showed up with a big turkey and plum pudding. Never ate so much in my life. All of us kids did. But then I knew it would be next Christmas before they came again, so I just hiked out of there."

"Where did you go?" asked Emily, picking up a little stick to guide Rufus into turning around. Then she amused herself by tracing letters in the dirt as she listened to Jackson.

"Well, I was on my own, just knockin' about, till the Child Catchers caught up with me and put me in a home where they used any excuse at all to beat me.

So I ran away again, and this time when I was caught, they dropped me off at the Overhill Stagecoach Company with a ticket to the West. Some family out there wants to put me to work." He looked at Emily's scribbles. "What you writing?"

"My mother's name," Emily said. "Constance Wiggins. And here's the name of the woman we lived with. . . ." She drew in the dirt some more. "Luella Nash."

"I don't know my letters," said Jackson. "All I can read is my own name. Never stayed in any place long enough to learn."

J-a-c-k-s-o-n, Emily wrote in the dirt.

"That's it," said Jackson. "How do you spell *your* name?"

E-m-i-l-y, she wrote.

"Funny-lookin' name," said Jackson. And then, "What do you want to do now?"

"What I really want to do is sleep," said Emily. "I was bumped and kicked all night long. I could curl up right here."

"Go ahead," said Jackson. "I'll see you around,

then." He got up and started to leave, then stopped. "Thank you for the breakfast."

"You're welcome," Emily told him. She put Rufus back in his box, then curled up in the hay and fell asleep.

• • •

The sun was fully up, carriages came and went, and still Emily slept on, exhausted from her travels. She slept all of the morning and part of the afternoon.

She was dreaming of cinnamon toast and hot cocoa when the barn door burst open and Jackson came in.

"Hey, Emily!" he called proudly. "I read your name!"

Slowly she sat up and rubbed her eyes. "What?"

"I saw your name! It's there in the newspaper up on the porch."

"How can that be?" asked Emily. "Did it say Emily Wiggins?"

"All I knew was the word *Emily,*" said Jackson.

Emily left Rufus and her carpetbag in the barn and

went back to the inn with Jackson. They made their way through the people coming and going. They went up onto the porch, stepped over a sleeping dog, squeezed between the rocking chairs, and looked at the newspaper pinned to the wall. Jackson pointed to a story at the top of the page.

"What does it say?" he asked her.

Emily was too surprised to answer. There in big black letters was the story:

Girl to Inherit Fortune

Emily Wiggins, daughter of a woman who worked for the late Luella Nash, will inherit ten million dollars. Constance Wiggins, who died in a carriage accident along with her wealthy employer, was the sole beneficiary of the Nash estate. She had only one child, a girl named Emily, eight years old, who will

now inherit her mother's fortune. Lawyers for the estate are trying to find her. Emily has long brown hair and green eyes and is believed to be on her way to Redbud.

"Is that *you*?" asked Jackson, pointing to the word *Emily.*

"Yes," said Emily, and in a voice weak with surprise, she softly read the story aloud to him.

"Ten million *dollars*?" Jackson whispered in astonishment.

"I . . . I guess so," said Emily. She was not sure just how much money that would be. One million, she guessed, was a lot of thousands, and *ten* million . . . She wondered if she could squeeze it all into the carpetbag.

"What are you going to *do* with all that money?" Jackson asked, looking around to make sure no one else was listening.

"I'll give it to Aunt Hilda, for taking me in," Emily replied. "Maybe I can buy her a horse and carriage. Do you think ten million is enough for a horse?"

"A horse!" Jackson exclaimed. "It's enough for a *ranch*!" Grabbing her by the arm, Jackson led her back down the steps and over to the shade of an oak tree. "Listen, Emily," he said. "A lot of people will be looking for you."

"That's good, isn't it?" Emily answered.

"But some of them might be the wrong kind of people," Jackson said. "And they'll be looking for you for the wrong reason."

Emily did not understand. She had lived all her life in the big white house, so she didn't know much about the world. But if people were looking for her, it was to tell her about the money, wasn't it?

"Everyone will try to be your friend, Emily, because they'll want some of that money," Jackson explained. "I think you should get to your aunt Hilda's before you tell anyone who you are. If people find out . . . well . . . you might not get to your aunt Hilda's at all."

Now, what in the hokie smokies could <u>that</u> mean?

SIX
Followed

This was truly alarming news, and Emily was frightened.

"Jackson, what do you mean?" she said. "Why wouldn't people want to help me?"

"Because they might want to help themselves more. The lawyers want to find you so they can give you the ten million; that's good. But what if someone kidnapped you and wouldn't give you up till he got the money? That's bad. A lot of folks might be looking for the girl with the brown hair and green eyes, which is you."

Glancing around to be sure no one was paying attention, Jackson yanked the newspaper off the wall and held it behind him.

But Emily was still upset. "What am I going to do?" she cried. "There must be newspapers in other places, and people will have seen them. When we get on the stagecoach, they'll guess who I am."

What would the neighbor women suggest? she wondered.

Mrs. Ready would say: "The wrong sort of people might be looking for her."

Mrs. Aim would ask: "So how can she hide until she gets to Redbud?"

And before Emily could think what Mrs. Fire might answer, Jackson grabbed her arm.

"Come on," he said, and pulled her back to the barn. There he crumpled the newspaper and hid it under the hay.

"Here's what we'll do," he said, taking a pair of

sheep shears off a hook on the wall. "I'll cut your hair short to make you look like a boy, and you can have one of my shirts, my cap, and a pair of britches."

"But . . . but it's all you have!" Emily said, looking at the small parcel he carried under his arm, knowing it could not hold much more than that.

"It's all right," said Jackson. "You shared your lunch with me, didn't you? When the Child Catchers get me again, they'll give me another set. They always give you more clothes, new or not, when they send you off to a different family." He held up the shears. "Ready? Should we do it?"

Oh, dear! Emily thought. *If only the neighbor women were here.*

"If she looks like a boy, it might keep the lawyers from finding her and giving her the money," Mrs. Ready might say worriedly.

"But if people know who she is and she's traveling alone, isn't she putting herself in danger?" Mrs. Aim might ask.

And Emily felt sure she knew what Mrs. Fire would

say: "Then let her look like a boy till she gets to Redbud, and her aunt will sort it out."

She had to trust someone, and one thing she did know: Aunt Hilda had invited her to come and live with her before she knew anything about the ten million dollars. And Jackson, despite his teasing, had been her friend too before he knew about her fortune.

Might as well get it over with.

"Ready," she said, taking off her bonnet. . . . She sat down on a wooden box. "Aim," she said. . . . And then, holding perfectly still, "Fire."

Jackson took the shears and began.

Snip, snip, snip, went the shears. Locks of brown hair began falling down around Emily's shoulders. *Snip, snip, snip,* the shears went again. Around her head, behind her ears, across her forehead. *Snip, snip . . . snip, snip . . .* When Jackson had finished, Emily's head felt very cool indeed, and when she ran her fingers through her hair, all her curls were gone. She swallowed.

"Okay. Now the clothes," said Jackson. "Here." He opened his parcel, and out fell a pair of britches and a shirt without a collar. He gave them both to Emily, as well as the cap on his head.

"I've got to go help the innkeeper if I want any extra for supper tonight," he said. "Change into my clothes, and when you come out, I'm going to call you Eli."

And Jackson went away.

Emily slipped off her dress and petticoat and put them and her bonnet at the bottom of her carpetbag. Then she put on Jackson's faded yellow shirt. It wasn't exactly clean. She pulled on his britches. They were rough and scratchy, but they fit. A pair of blue suspenders hung from the waistband, and she slipped them over her shoulders. Her own socks and shoes were gray, so they did not seem to matter. Finally she put on Jackson's cap. Then she left her bag and Rufus's box and started for the inn.

The innkeeper was looking around. "Here, lad!" he called when he saw her. "Could you carry this hatbox into the parlor for the lady in the red dress?"

Emily was relieved that he mistook her for a boy. "Sure," she said. She took the large hatbox from the innkeeper and followed the woman in the red dress into the tavern and over to the parlor.

"Thank you, son," said the woman, giving Emily a nickel. "Just set it there on the table."

Emily dropped the nickel in the pocket of her

britches. On her way out again, she stopped for a moment to look at herself in the big mirror next to the staircase.

A boy of eight stared back at her. A boy with short straggly hair, wearing a cap down over his eyes, a faded yellow shirt, and brown britches with blue suspenders.

"Hello, Eli," Emily whispered to her reflection, and tried to walk like a boy as she went outside. She took bigger strides. She swung her arms. She jumped down the last two steps, and even tried to whistle.

"Hey, Eli! Want to climb a tree out there by the pasture?" called Jackson.

He began to run, and Emily followed. It was easier to run in britches, she discovered—even scratchy britches that made her itch—than it was to run with a skirt and petticoat twisting about her legs.

They reached the pasture and straddled the fence. This time Emily climbed up all by herself. After she made it onto the first branch of the big tree, the second seemed a bit easier. And after she hoisted herself onto the second branch, the third was easier still.

There she sat, looking out over the fields, her feet dangling five yards off the ground.

Jackson grinned at her. "How do you like it?" he asked.

"I like it fine!" said Emily, beaming. "If my mother could have worn britches, she would have liked it too." She looked at Jackson. "Do you miss your mother?"

Jackson turned away. "Nope," he said. "She was never around much for me to miss. I miss my pa, though. What about you?"

"I miss my mother every day," said Emily, her eyes tearing up. But she had a home to go to now, and she would soon be living with her aunt Hilda.

• • •

Emily stayed in the shadows as much as she could that afternoon, watching the children in other families as they arrived or departed Callaway's Inn. Boys, she noticed, liked to push and punch each other. They jumped up and down. They took off their jackets and used them to wallop each other over the head.

When the innkeeper needed help, both Jackson and

Emily volunteered. As visitors slid down off their saddles, Jackson tied up the horses. He carried bags and even babies up the steps to the parlor. Emily swept the porch and brought in wood for the stove box. There were so many children about that the innkeeper didn't know one from another.

When it was close to suppertime, Emily felt hungry and went inside to see if the food was ready. She wound her way through the people milling about in the hallway, and almost bumped into a man who was standing at the bar, a glass of whiskey in his hand.

The man wore black boots up to the knee, brown britches, and a brown shirt. The sleeves of his shirt were rolled up to his elbows; his large arms bulged out of his sleeves, and on one of the huge arms was . . . a tiger tattoo.

And who in the freakin' frazzles

do you figure he was?

SEVEN

Hiding

Emily's heart thumped loudly—so loudly she was almost afraid that the man could hear it. Ducking behind the grandfather clock, she slowly raised her eyes to the person there at the bar. He was talking to the man next to him. She remembered the silver-black hair of a wolf, the eyes of a weasel. And when he spoke, Emily recognized the voice of the uncle she had hoped never to see again.

"Where am I going?" Uncle Victor said, his voice

a growl. "Well, as luck would have it, I'm about to come into a bit of money, and I'm looking for my poor orphaned niece to share it with."

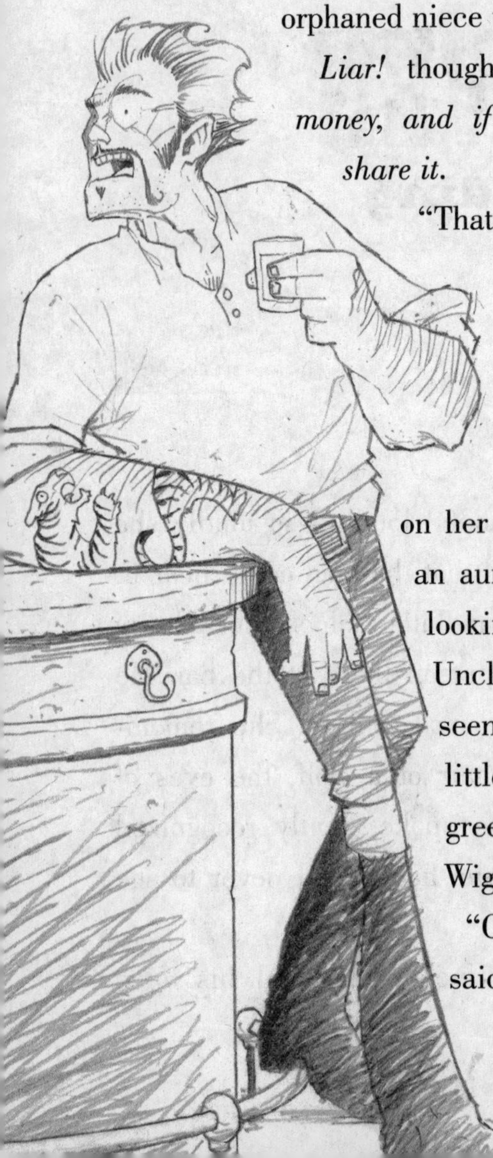

Liar! thought Emily. *It's not your money, and if it were, you wouldn't share it.*

"That's mighty nice of you," the other man said. "Some folks wouldn't lift a finger to help a poor orphaned niece."

"Heard she might be on her way to Redbud to visit an aunt, so thought I'd come looking for her here first," Uncle Victor said. "Haven't seen her, have you? Small little thing, long brown hair, green eyes? Name of Emily Wiggins."

"Can't say that I have," said the man next to him.

"Just got here myself, but the place is crawling with kids."

Emily almost tripped over her own feet as she hurried, breathless, out to the porch again. Men were talking, women were rocking their babies, and children chased each other around the yard.

"Jackson," Emily cried, grabbing his arm. "He's here!"

"Who?" asked Jackson.

"The person who wants to be my friend for the wrong reason," Emily panted. And she told him about her uncle Victor, who had never said a kind word. "I heard him tell someone that he's come into a bit of money, and I know he means mine! He said he's looking for his niece, Emily Wiggins."

"Did he see you?" Jackson asked.

Emily shook her head. "He said that his orphaned niece

was on her way to Redbud, and asked if anyone had seen me. What am I going to *do*?"

"Would he recognize you if he saw you?" Jackson asked.

"I don't know," Emily told him. She'd been six years old when she'd last seen her uncle, the year she'd received her turtle. In those last two years she had lost her baby teeth, and she had grown a bit slimmer and taller—but *she* certainly recognized *him*.

"Then here's what we'll do," said Jackson. "I heard that the next stagecoach gets in tomorrow at ten. You'll sleep in the barn tonight in case your uncle sticks around, and as soon as the coach arrives, we're on it. Okay?"

"Okay," said Emily.

Just at that moment the screen door opened and down the steps came the man with the tiger tattoo. He didn't look left and he didn't look right. He came directly over to Jackson and Emily, and Emily's knees shook so hard she could feel them knock together.

"What are you kids doing here?" Uncle Victor growled.

"Just helping out, earn a nickel now and then," Jackson answered.

"What are your names?" asked the man with the tiger tattoo.

"I'm Jackson, and this here is my brother Eli. But he don't talk so good," Jackson said. "Got kicked in the head by a mule when he was three."

Emily did not know how Jackson could think up a story so fast, but she was glad he was doing the talking. She tried to keep her eyes on the ground, but every so often they traveled up the black boots to the brown pant legs, up the brown pant legs to the shirt, and up the shirt to the face, where the eyebrows came together over the bridge of the nose. And each time she looked up, her uncle's eyes were fastened on her.

"Didn't happen to see a girl named Emily around here, did you?" Uncle Victor asked. "Innkeeper thinks there was a girl here going to Redbud, but she gave up her seat to somebody else."

"Yes, sir, I did," said Jackson. "Her and a boy both was going on the stagecoach, and they gave up their seats. But at the last minute they squeezed the girl in after all."

Uncle Victor looked angry. "If that was her, she's probably halfway there by now," he said, scowling.

"I'd bet your boots for mine, if I had any," said Jackson. "But I don't think it was Redbud where she was going. Someplace else. Can't remember."

"Well, *try*!" Uncle Victor said, glaring at him.

Jackson cupped his chin in his hand. "Hmmm," he said. "Fort somethin', maybe? Or was it a city?" He brightened a little. "A river town, that was it!" And then, "Naw. Don't think so."

"Oh, you're no help!" Uncle Victor growled, and moved on to ask someone else.

Emily's legs almost gave way beneath her. "He won't stop looking for me until I'm found!" she whispered.

Just at that moment a carriage pulled up to the door of the inn. On the door was painted:

CATCHUM CHILD-CATCHING
SERVICES
CALLAWAY DIVISION

"The barn!" Jackson whispered, and he and Emily ran as fast as they could to the hay-smelling darkness of the old barn.

"They're on your trail now, Emily," Jackson said. "Everybody in the country will want to find a girl worth ten million dollars. Half of 'em will want to help you get it, and the other half will want to take it away."

"How do you know that?" Emily asked. "How could people be so cruel?"

"Not cruel as much as greedy," Jackson said. "I've been around. I can smell a rat a block away. I can smell a skunk a mile away. I can tell when the Catchum folks'll be here before you even hear the carriage. The lawyers will pay them plenty to have you found so they can get things settled, get their own money, and close the case."

Emily was quiet for a long time. Finally she asked in a very small voice, "Then how do I know *you're* not out to trick me, Jackson?"

"If I was out to get your money, I'd tell that uncle of yours where he could find you, providing he'd split the money with me when he got it," Jackson said.

Emily was growing wiser faster than she ever imagined, because she heard herself say, "But how do I know that's not just what you're planning to do?"

"You don't, I guess," said Jackson. "But I know what it's like to be alone in the world. I know what it's like to have folks after you too." And then he asked, "You hungry?"

"A little," said Emily.

"I'm going up to the inn for my supper, and I'll bring some to you," Jackson said. "If I don't come back right away, it'll mean somebody's got their eye on me, and I'll have to find another way to sneak to the barn."

"The Child Catchers wouldn't take you, would they, Jackson?" Emily asked.

"Naw. I'm doing what they want—heading west. I'll be out of their hair and into someone else's, and they won't have to bother about me anymore," he said.

"Please be careful anyway," Emily told him. "You're the only friend I have besides Rufus."

But how in the ding-dong dickens could she really trust him?

EIGHT
A Horrible, Terrible Thought

Jackson peeked through the door and quietly slipped outside.

Fifteen minutes went by. An hour, perhaps. Emily had no way to tell time. All at once she heard the thud of boots in the back of the barn. She quickly burrowed down in the hay, using handfuls to cover herself and her carpetbag.

What if Jackson had told her uncle where she was hiding? What if he'd brought the Child Catchers too, and Emily was trapped in the barn? They would send her off to live with Uncle Victor, she was sure of it, for he would be on his best behavior before a judge. No one would believe her stories of his unkindness, no one but Mrs. Ready, Mrs. Aim, and Mrs. Fire.

But the noise was only the stable boy bringing in the cow for the night, and after he left, Jackson slipped through the big open doorway of the barn and pulled a muffin from one pocket, a pork chop from another.

"Sorry I'm so late," he said, "but your uncle was talking to the Child Catcher folks, and I wanted to hear what they were saying."

Emily sat up, took the food he offered, and hungrily began to eat. "What *were* they saying?" she asked.

"Your uncle's angry because the Child Catchers haven't found you, and the Catchum folks said they'd keep trying. They finally got back in their carriage and rode off. I think your uncle's going to move along too."

"Oh, I hope so!" said Emily.

The full moon shone through the doorway of the barn, leaving a patch of golden light just inside the entrance. Jackson soon fell asleep with his head on his arm. Emily finished eating and burrowed deep down in the hay next to the wall. She woke once when someone came into the barn to milk the cow and take it out to pasture. But when she woke again, the sun was up, and Jackson was shaking her by the shoulder.

"Get yourself ready, Emily," he said. "Get all the hay out of your hair, and remember: from now on, you're my brother, but don't say anything unless you have to. Stay here in the barn, and as soon as you hear the bugle, come running. We'll be first in line for the coach."

He gave her the biscuit and apple he had brought for her, and then he left. Emily let Rufus crawl around while she ate her breakfast, for who knew when her little turtle would have the next chance to leave his box?

Halfway through the morning, there it was: the stagecoach driver's bugle. Emily jumped to her feet and grabbed the carpetbag with Rufus in it, and with the legs of Jackson's britches smacking against each other as she ran, she managed to get to the front of the line beside her friend.

The passengers who had traveled to Callaway got off, and Emily and Jackson got on. The driver checked their tickets and pointed to the backseat. An old man climbed on next and sat beside them.

A plump woman and her grown sister pulled each other up into the coach and, seeing Emily and Jackson in back, said they hoped the children would behave themselves and sit quietly without a lot of squirming. Then they plopped themselves down in the middle seat.

Finally three rumpled men took the front seat, facing backward toward the women, changing places with each other three times to decide who would get to sit by a window.

How could she possibly sit still all the way to Redbud? Emily wondered. Her legs would go to sleep! Her feet would be numb! But she waited patiently as the other passengers shuffled their belongings. A bag bumped Emily on the head. A box fell off a shelf and banged her knees. The stagecoach creaked. It dipped and swayed as the passengers arranged themselves, and the horses, eager to be off, pawed at the ground and snorted impatiently.

They want to get going as much as I do, thought Emily. *Go! Just go!*

The driver in the blue jacket with the gold buttons climbed up to the seat atop the coach, and Emily waited for the bugle. People gathered on the porch of Callaway's Inn to see them go, and a last-minute stack of mail was delivered to the back of the stagecoach to take to the people out west.

The doors closed. The horses snorted again. But just before the stagecoach started to move, a man with silver-black hair and weasel eyes and a tiger tattoo on his forearm came running from the inn and leaped up onto the seat beside the driver. The bugle blew, and off they went.

Emily felt as though she could not breathe.

As the other passengers cried, "We're off!" and waved goodbye, she turned and stared at Jackson. Was this a trick? Had he known all along that Uncle Victor was going with them? But Jackson looked worried too.

"It's okay, Eli," he whispered. "If he knew it was

you, he would have grabbed you back at the inn."

"Gracious sakes!" said one plump sister, her orange curls bobbing as she spoke. "Wonder who's the handsome man in the black boots, riding up there beside the driver?"

The first of the rumpled-looking men facing her answered, "It's my guess he bribed the driver, because *no*body rides up there without an invitation."

"Back at Callaway's, he said he was looking for a runaway niece," said the second man. "He thinks she might have got off at Fort Jawbone. Going to look for her there, I guess."

"But, my! Doesn't he have a fine mustache!" said the second grown sister, who had bright painted lips. "We're on our way to Redbud. How far are you three men going?"

"We're heading west to dig for gold," bragged the third man. "Oscar, Angus, and Jock, that's us, and I'm Jock. Who might you ladies be?" He lifted his shirt and scratched his belly.

The sister with the orange hair made a face and held

a handkerchief to her nose. But the sister with the bright red lips answered, "I'm Petunia and she's Marigold." And then, to be polite, she turned around and asked the old man behind her his name.

"Eh?" said the old man next to Emily, cupping one hand to his ear.

"What's your name?" asked Petunia, more loudly.

"Muffit," he shouted back as though no one else could hear either. "Mortimer Muffit." And he nodded off.

No one seemed the least bit interested in learning the children's names, because as Luella Nash used to say, children were best seen and not heard.

As Marigold and Petunia turned their attention to the window, the three rumpled men began talking among themselves.

"How long you figure before we get to Deadman's Belch?" Jock asked the others. "That'll be the halfway point."

"Not Belch, stupid," said Oscar. "Gulch! Deadman's Gulch."

"It's a long way yet," said Angus. "Got to go through

Snakeville and Bull's Eye, then down Lantern Hill to the ferry."

Emily hardly knew what she was afraid of most. She was glad to be leaving Callaway so the Catchum Child Catchers couldn't get her. But even the thought of Deadman's Gulch or a place called Snakeville wasn't as frightening as the thought of living with Uncle Victor for the rest of her life. She felt sure that he would send her off to a horrid boarding school while he went to work spending her money. She had heard the servants talk about such things back in Miss Nash's big white house, for they had worked in other places.

To comfort herself, Emily took Rufus out of his box and let him crawl around in her lap. The good thing about sitting in the last row was that the people in front of her couldn't see her turtle. The old man beside them opened one eye and watched for a minute, then nodded off again.

Jackson was swinging his legs and accidentally kicked the back of the seat in front of him. Marigold cast a scolding look over her shoulder and said to her sister, "For charity's sake, I hope that fine man in the black boots finds his niece, but if he does, he'd better not try to squeeze her in here. Two squirming children are enough."

Emily cupped her hands over Rufus to hide him.

"And what *are* your names, boys?" Marigold asked.

"I'm Jackson and he's Eli," Jackson answered.

"Well, just don't do a lot of squirming back there," the woman said. "Your brother seems a bit shy, if not backward, but let's hope he doesn't whine." She turned forward once again.

What Emily had hoped was that once she left Callaway's Inn and her uncle behind, she could be Emily again. That in one of the way stations, she could change out of Jackson's scratchy britches and put on her dress and petticoat. That she could take off Jackson's cap and cover her short scruffy hair with the little blue bonnet.

Now she knew she would have to go on being Eli for a long time. How could she keep pretending that she had been kicked in the head by a mule?

As the stagecoach bounced along, Emily began to realize that the backseat was probably the most uncomfortable of the three benches, for she felt every bump in the road. When the coach turned a corner, however, everyone was tossed this way and that.

Once, when the horses made a particularly sharp turn, the three rumpled men fell over on each other.

"Your boot's on my foot!" complained Jock.

"Your foot's on my leg!" said Angus.

"And your leg's in my lap!" said Oscar, pushing them back into place.

After many hours and many new teams of horses, the stagecoach stopped long enough for the passengers to go inside a way station for a quick supper of beans and biscuits.

"C'mon, Eli, get some supper," Jackson said loudly as he climbed out of the stagecoach, wanting Uncle Victor to hear.

Silently, Emily followed behind Jackson, her eyes hidden beneath the flat cap, but once inside, when she finally looked up, she found she was sitting directly across from her uncle at the table.

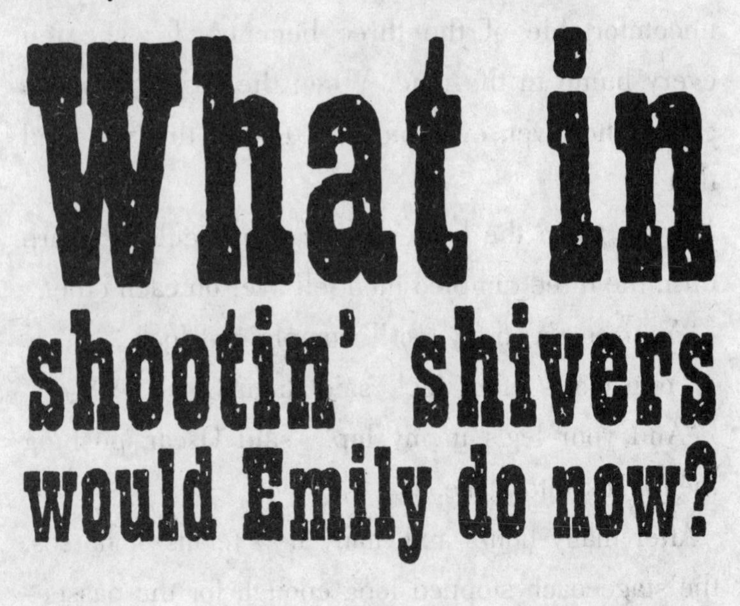

NINE
Fever

"Didn't know you boys would be aboard," Uncle Victor said, in a voice like a rumble of thunder.

"Didn't ask us," said Jackson, reaching for a biscuit.

"Where you headed?" Uncle Victor asked.

"Don't rightly know," Jackson answered. "Figure the driver'll tell us where to get off."

"Now, that's strange," said the man with the tiger tattoo. "Even orphans should have some idea of where they're going."

"It's all I can do to keep track of my brother," said Jackson. "Figure we'll get there soon enough."

"What's wrong with the lad?" asked Oscar from his end of the table.

"Got kicked in the head by a horse," said Jackson. "Never been right since."

"Thought you told me it was a mule," said Uncle Victor.

Thumpa thumpa thumpa, went Emily's heart.

"Horse . . . mule . . . whatever it was. I weren't there. Just heard our ma screamin', and from then on, he could never speak a word," Jackson explained.

"Well, they ought not to send children out on the road by themselves, orphans or not," said Marigold. "Something happened to them, who would ever know?"

Who indeed? Emily had another terrible, horrible thought: if something *did* happen to her, the ten million dollars would go to Uncle Victor, wouldn't it? *He* would be the next of kin. Just a simple little accident out here in the night and, as Jackson had said, she might not get to Redbud at all.

• • •

It was dark after they'd finished eating. When they went back to the coach, the driver had turned down the backs of the three benches so that there was one large platform where all eight people could sleep—nine now, including the man with the tiger tattoo. The drivers had changed, and the new one wanted no one up there beside him as they rode.

This, Emily found, was even worse than sleeping four or five to a bed at Callaway's Inn. There wasn't room to turn over, and each time the coach hit a rock or a tree root, her head rose from the floor and banged back down again. The two sisters groaned and complained, but the elderly man was squeezed against one end of the coach and seemed to be sleeping soundly.

About midnight, they neared Lantern Hill. When they reached the top, the driver sounded several notes on his bugle to announce their approach to the ferryman, who would carry them across the river. But the horses were so eager for a drink that they galloped all the way down the steep hill. On top of the coach, trunks slid this way and that. Inside the coach, bodies rolled and bumped against each other.

"Get your elbow out of my belly!" Oscar yelled to Angus.

And Angus yelled to Jock, "Get your backside out of my face!"

The stagecoach, in fact, was a bit top-heavy. When it stopped, the ferryman ordered all the men and boys out to help guide it onto the raft.

"You too, Eli," Jackson whispered, and Emily, who was sleepily rubbing her eyes, climbed out beside Jackson.

The ferryman slowly led the nervous horses onto the raft. He told the men and boys to stand along the back and sides of the coach to make sure it didn't tip over once they started across the river.

Emily felt a chill as she and Uncle Victor passed each other in the darkness. For a moment she stumbled, but she managed to catch herself before she fell into the river. And she thought about how easy, how very easy, it would be for Uncle Victor to get rid of her forever if he knew who she really was.

• • •

It was early morning when they reached Fort Jawbone, and all the passengers went inside. Emily was wide awake now. She nervously waited for Uncle Victor to find out that Emily Wiggins was not there. Then, perhaps, he would give up the chase and go home, wherever that was.

As they ate the cold meal that was provided for them, Angus said, "Better eat hearty, mates. Last good meal we'll have for a long while, you can bet."

"It'll be beans and bacon from here to California," added Oscar.

"And maybe some wormy bread," put in Jock,

wiggling his fingers. Emily was glad she wasn't going all the way to California.

But Uncle Victor wasn't interested in eating. Emily watched him go from one person to the next at Fort Jawbone, asking if anyone there remembered an eight-year-old passenger by the name of Emily Wiggins who had come through on a stagecoach two days before.

"Can't say that I do," one of the workers told him. "We get a few orphans now and then on their way out west, but I don't remember that there was a young girl on the last coach."

"Well," growled Uncle Victor. "Maybe she didn't come through, then, or maybe she's given me the slip. I'll have to go on to Redbud and see if I can find her there."

Emily's breath seemed caught in her throat, and she almost choked on a biscuit.

No! No! She could not stand it! Riding with Uncle Victor three more days and three more nights, pretending to be a boy? How would she go that long without speaking? Would she even have a voice once she got to Aunt Hilda's? But again it was time to board.

"Eli!" Jackson called. "Come on!"

A new driver leaped up to the driver's seat and the whip cracked. Sitting in the back again, Emily fed Rufus a fly Jackson had caught, and looked into his tiny face.

"Dear little friend," she whispered. "Only a few more days and I'll never put you in a box again. We'll be at Aunt Hilda's and you'll have all the grass you want. I'll make you your own little pool, and the sun will shine on you every day."

Rufus looked up at her and blinked his eyes. He crawled over to the old man's leg, and Mortimer Muffit didn't even notice.

"We're off!" Jock chortled as the carriage rattled across the ground.

"No turnin' back now!" said Angus.

"We're headed for Deadman's Gulch, and the best part of the trip's behind us," said Oscar.

But the two grown sisters were all aflutter because the tall man with the tiger tattoo was riding inside the coach now, on the very bench where they were sitting, the only spot left.

"Oh, Mr. Victor!" Marigold purred, adjusting her bonnet. "I do love the way your mustache curls."

"And *I* love the way your shiny boots shine!" crooned Petunia.

"Uh . . . thank you, ladies," Uncle Victor said without smiling.

"And that tiger tattoo!" exclaimed Marigold.

"Did you actually kill a tiger?" asked Petunia.

"Not exactly," said Uncle Victor uncomfortably, and turned his attention to the window.

Jackson poked Emily with his elbow and Emily *almost* smiled. She was afraid of Uncle Victor, and Uncle Victor was afraid of the ladies.

As the coach went on, the land became rocky and rough. There was a way station every twenty miles or so, where passengers were allowed to get out and eat. Each time, Emily and Jackson finished before the others, then went outside and chased each other around. Jackson ran as fast as he could, first one way, then another, while Emily worked to keep up.

Back in Luella Nash's big house with the flowers planted just so, the bushes clipped, the walks swept, the leaves raked, and the grass mowed, one did not hop, skip, or jump. One did not skid, slither, or slide. And one *especially* did not run. But after a while, Emily discovered that her legs were stronger than she'd thought. She was glad of the exercise before the coach started out again.

"Oh, Mr. Tiger Man," said Marigold playfully as evening settled down over the prairie. "Tell us about your adventures hunting tigers!"

"Yes, yes!" said Petunia with a giggle. "I get all tingly when I think of tigers. Lions too. Tell us, have you ever shot a lion?"

Uncle Victor edged even closer to the window. "Ladies," he said, "I believe you are misinformed."

This time Emily poked Jackson as they sat on the backseat and listened.

"*We* will believe anything you tell us!" said Petunia. "We do *love* a good story!"

"*I'll* tell you a good story!" said Jock, who was sitting across from them. "You ever hear about the Ghost of Pimple Pass?" He scratched his nose with one hand and his knee with the other.

"*Prickly* Pass, you idiot," said Angus.

"No ghost there at all, you imbecile," said Oscar. "You're thinking of the Ghost of Phantom Hill."

Angus gave Oscar's arm a slap. "Weren't no hill at all. That's the creek you're thinkin' of, Phantom Creek, where we found some gold our first trip out."

At this Jock hee-hawed like a donkey. "And it weren't no new gold in that creek at all. Just my gold tooth that fell in the water."

"Well, if you're not going to tell the story, I will," said Oscar. "It was the Ghost of Phantom Hill, sure as I'm sittin' here. And it was all because of the severed hand that was found at Killer's Grave."

"*What?*" cried Petunia. "A severed hand?"

"There it was," Angus interrupted. "Just lyin' atop the grave, cut clean off at the wrist. Many a murder's taken place in these parts, and they say if you go through Prickly Pass when the moon is full and you hear this moanin' off in the bushes . . ."

Petunia shrieked and clutched Uncle Victor's arm as Marigold reached across her and grabbed his knee.

"Ladies!" Uncle Victor cried, prying their hands

loose and flattening himself against the window.

"If you ever hear a moanin', it's likely to be an old coyote got itself a bellyache," finished Jock with a laugh.

Angus glared at him. ". . . it'll be the ghost comin' back to look for his hand," he finished.

At that very moment, as the coach was about to ford a creek, the rain that had begun that afternoon became a downpour. The driver called for all the men and boys to push the coach out of the mud.

Uncle Victor seemed glad of a chance to escape the women, and hurriedly opened the door. Out Emily jumped, along with Jackson. Her feet sank ankle-deep in mud and her little boots filled with water.

"Push! Push!" the driver yelled, and Emily and Jackson put their shoulders against the coach, along with Oscar, Angus, and Jock. Old Mr. Muffit got out to see what was going on, turning up the collar of his jacket.

Uncle Victor was up front with the driver, whipping the horses to make them go. At last, with a huge sucking sound, the stagecoach rose up out of the mud. The dirty men and boys (and Emily) crawled back into the coach to wipe themselves off as best they could, and finally the coach was off again.

Emily had gone so long without speaking that she was almost getting used to being quiet. But as the gold-digging men continued their stories of the strange things that had happened on their first journey out west, it was hard not to ask questions. And when Oscar began a story about a skull on top of a high rock, she looked at the elderly man to see if he believed it. She wasn't sure, but for a moment one eye seemed open and one eye closed; then he seemed to be sleeping again as usual.

But the man with the tiger tattoo wasn't sleepy, and he told no tales. Emily was already shivering in her wet and muddy clothes. And in the near darkness inside the stagecoach, when Uncle Victor turned his head to look out the window, his face had such an angry, scheming look that she shivered all the more.

• • •

The next morning, Jackson wasn't saying much either, because he had come down with a fever. When

Emily's arm touched his, she could tell that his skin was warm beneath his shirt, and his lips looked parched.

"Mercy, I hope he doesn't have something that will bring us all down!" Marigold said worriedly. She and Petunia traded places with the children so that Jackson could have a bit more air on the middle bench.

Emily let her lap be Jackson's pillow. Mr. Moffit and the two sisters leaned over the seat and fanned the boy. Oscar, Angus, and Jock kept Jackson's tin cup filled with water from their own jug. But the man with the tiger tattoo only watched from his end of the row.

Sometimes Jackson moved his lips and sometimes he asked for more water. But once, when he opened his eyes and saw Emily wiping his face with a wet cloth, he said, "Emily. . . ."

Startled, she put one finger over his lips. *Thumpa thumpa thumpa,* went her heart. The two sisters continued fanning. Oscar, Angus, and Jock had fallen asleep, and so had the elderly man. But Uncle Victor stared hard at Emily, the pupils of his eyes as small and dark as those of a rat.

What in the hunky monkey do you suppose he was thinking?

TEN

Trouble

The next day, Jackson was feeling better, and he and Emily took their seats in the back row once again.

"You were right sick there for a while, son," Oscar said. "Good thing you had your brother to care for you. He was worried about you, even though his brain's not all there. Time or two you called out for someone named Emily."

Emily saw Jackson's eyes widen with alarm. "Guess I was dreamin' about our ma," he said quickly.

"Where *is* your mother?" asked Petunia.

"She's passed, ma'am. Died when I was six. And we've been bounced around from pillar to post ever since," Jackson said.

Emily was amazed at the stories Jackson could tell. He had told *her* that his ma had run off. She wondered if *any* of his stories were true.

"Two little orphan boys, alone in the world," Marigold murmured, and sighed as she turned her attention once more to the window.

Emily stole a look at her uncle, but she couldn't tell from his weasel eyes whether he believed Jackson or not. If only she could get to Redbud before he discovered who she was! There had been so many fresh teams of horses, so many different drivers.

She imagined the big red stagecoach pulling up to the Redbud way station. She could almost feel Aunt Hilda's arms around her. But each time Emily looked up from her daydream, the man with the tiger tattoo was watching . . . watching out the window as though he might see his niece crouched behind a rock, a tree. Watching the way stations to see if she'd been dropped off there. Watching Jackson and Emily when they ate their meals. Watching . . .

There was only a trace of a road in desert country, and here and there a lone tree. Sagebrush took the place of bushes, and large outcroppings of rocks stood in place of buildings. The latest driver was young and impatient. He ran the horses hard, eager to reach the next stop. But one of the wheels hit a rock, turning sharply; the frame broke, and over the stagecoach went, at the very edge of a deep ravine.

The door of the coach flew open, and everyone spilled out. Oscar and Angus and Jock and Uncle Victor hit the ground first. Marigold and Petunia fell on top of them, the elderly man found himself on top of Petunia, and when Jackson and Emily came tumbling out, Emily rolled off the heap of arms and legs and right over the edge of the cliff.

"Eli!" Jackson yelled.

The driver muttered as he picked himself up, more concerned about his wheel than his passengers, it seemed. The two sisters rubbed their bruised arms; Oscar and Angus and Jock massaged their twisted necks, and old Mr. Muffit seemed for a moment to have his beard on backward. But Jackson was peering over the edge of the cliff, looking for Emily, who had disappeared.

Emily herself hardly knew what was happening. Over and over she rolled, desperately trying to grab on to something. Small rocks were dislodged from the dry ground as she fell, and they rolled down on top of her.

Whop. A clump of earth hit her leg. *Ping.* A stone stung her cheek.

Finally she managed to clutch the root of a scraggly bush, and her feet found a resting place on a rock. Her arms were scratched and her leg was bleeding. Emily thought if she could only find her heart and get it back in her chest where it belonged, she might live. She could hear it beating in her head, her ears, her throat. And then she thought of Rufus.

Rufus! She had been holding the little box with her turtle in it, waiting for the next way station so she could sneak off and let him have some air and a walk. Where was the box? Frantically she looked about her.

The lid was at her feet, the box itself upside down on a ledge below. But where was Rufus?

How horrible to have come this far only to lose her little friend. Her eyes were so full of tears she could not see, and she leaned down and wiped them on her shoulder. "Rufus!" she whispered, holding tight to the bush as she looked all around. Something moved on the ledge below, and she recognized her pet.

"Eli!" came a hoarse call as Jackson appeared, dangling above her, holding on to a tree root. "Give me your hand!"

Emily only shook her head, and inch by inch she lowered herself down the side of the cliff.

A little farther, farther still . . . If she could climb down a maple tree, Emily told herself, she could do this. At last she reached Rufus. And as soon as she had the box and the turtle both, she thrust them into one of the deep pockets of her britches and grabbed hold of Jackson's outstretched hand as she made her way up again. The two of them climbed back to the top, where Oscar, Angus, and Jock helped pull them to safety.

Jackson was still pale from his fever, but he was more worried about Emily than himself. Uncle Victor, however, showed no interest in the rescue. While the two sisters fussed over the children and brushed off their clothes, Uncle Victor swore at the driver who had driven so recklessly and stood over him as he worked to repair the wheel.

"You're wasting my time," he growled. "I need to get to Redbud in a hurry."

"Well, breathin' down my neck ain't going to help you, mister," the driver said. "If I drive too slow, folks complain and want to get there sooner. If I drive too fast, they complain and want to get there safer. You can help the most by gettin' out of my way."

The man with the weasel eyes and the tiger tattoo swore again, but he went to stand in the shade of a large boulder, where he paced restlessly back and forth.

After she and Jackson had drunk some water, Emily began to feel a little better, and so did Jackson.

"For a minute there, I thought you were a goner!" he told Emily when Marigold and Petunia wandered off.

"I looked over the edge and it was a long way down to the bottom."

"I was scared too," Emily whispered. "But more scared of losing Rufus than anything."

The other passengers found what shade they could. The elderly man was resting. Oscar, Angus, and Jock were smoking their pipes. But Marigold and Petunia could not find a comfortable place to sit. They could not get back in the coach until it was upright, and it could not be upright until the driver had repaired the wheel. So they began to argue with each other.

"When we get back in the coach, I get to sit by the tiger man," Emily heard Marigold say. "You've been sitting by him ever since we woke up this morning. I saw him first, remember."

"What does it matter?" said Petunia. "That perfume you wear could knock an elephant over."

"What?" said Marigold. "Why, those silly flowers on top of your bonnet poke his cheek whenever you turn your head."

"Really!" said Petunia. "And who gave me this bonnet, may I ask?"

"Better to smell my perfume than smell your feet. Really, Petunia, you should keep your boots on in the carriage."

Emily and Jackson watched as the sisters turned their backs on each other, noses in the air. But the heat soon overtook the women and they began complaining about other things. They even complained about a herd of buffalo grazing not far away.

"That is surely the ugliest animal on the face of the earth," said Marigold.

"An animal that ugly should never have been born," agreed Petunia.

One of the buffalo moved toward the coach as it munched, a cloud of insects swarming above its huge furry hump.

"Get out of here, you ugly thing, you!" shouted Marigold.

"Leave it be," the driver called, trying to fit the repaired wheel back in place. "It's not doing you no harm."

"Well, it's smelly," said Petunia. "I can smell it from here. Probably has fleas and every kind of lice known to man." She picked up a stone and threw it at the animal. It studied her with its enormous eyes, then went on eating.

"Leave it be, I said," called the driver. "I'll have this wheel back on in a little while."

But Marigold picked up an even bigger stone and hurled it at the buffalo. It struck him on the nose. "Shooo!" she yelled. "Get!"

And suddenly, the buffalo lowered its head and charged.

Emily gasped as the big animal barreled toward the two sisters and knocked them down. Then it charged the driver, who dived behind the carriage. The buffalo turned around in circles, pawing the ground, and all Emily knew then was that her legs were moving, her feet were hitting the ground, and she and Jackson were running like the wind.

She had no trouble keeping up with him this time. Emily had never known she could run so fast. She ran so fast she couldn't think. All she knew was that she still had Rufus and his little box deep in one trouser pocket.

When Jackson told her at last that the buffalo had gone back to the herd, Emily collapsed to the ground and sat catching her breath while she and Jackson watched the uproar back by the stagecoach, and the scolding the two grown sisters got from the driver.

Fortunately, neither Marigold nor Petunia was seriously hurt. Their bonnets had been crushed and their clothes trampled, but at last the carriage was upright, the trunks and boxes were back in place, and everyone climbed aboard.

But inside the coach, passengers sniped at each other as the stagecoach took off again. Oscar and Angus called the two sisters insane; Marigold and Petunia said that the men's chewing tobacco made them sick; Uncle Victor told them all to quiet down, that he had some thinking to do; and Marigold patted his hand and said she would be as quiet as a little mouse sitting beside such a big handsome tiger man. Mr. Mortimer Muffit on the bench beside Emily and Jackson didn't seem to be quite himself, his beard awry, whiskers going in every direction.

"Are you all right?" Jackson asked him.

"Eh?" he said.

"Are you hurt?" Jackson asked.

The elderly man shook his head. "No," he said, and closed his eyes.

Emily was glad to be moving again, but she was still shaking inside. How quiet her life had been back in Luella Nash's big house. If only the kind neighbor women could be on the coach right now instead of the two fussy sisters; if only her dear mother were here instead of Uncle Victor, how much better a trip it would be. All she had now were Jackson and Rufus.

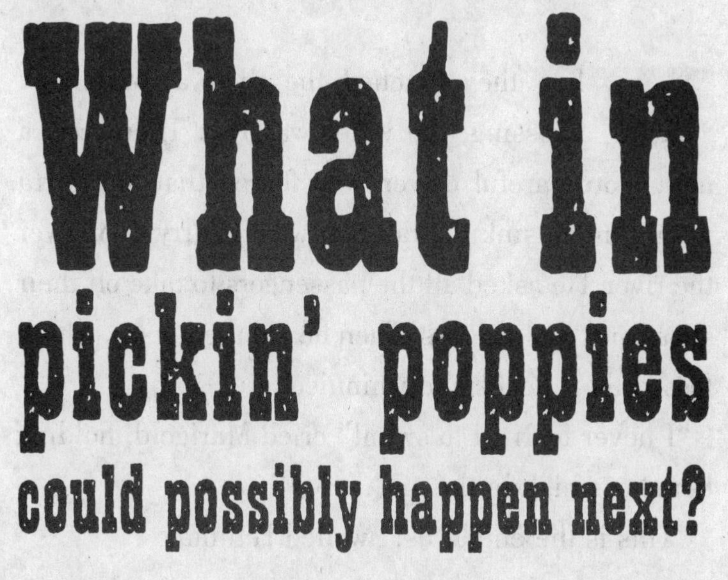

ELEVEN
The Secret Is Out

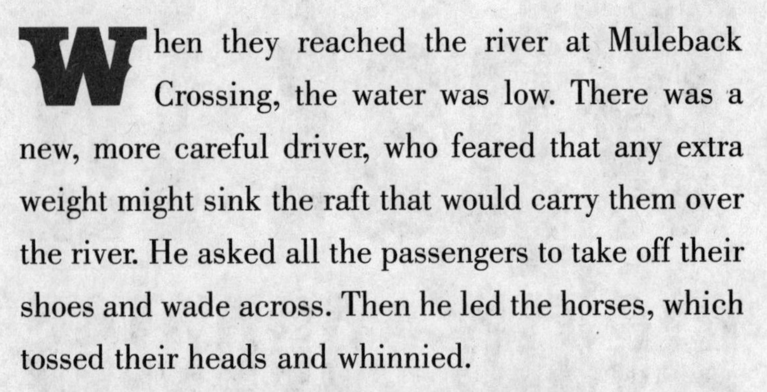

When they reached the river at Muleback Crossing, the water was low. There was a new, more careful driver, who feared that any extra weight might sink the raft that would carry them over the river. He asked all the passengers to take off their shoes and wade across. Then he led the horses, which tossed their heads and whinnied.

"I never learned to swim!" cried Marigold, holding her shoes high in the air.

"This is the end of us!" wailed Petunia.

"Don't I wish," said Oscar gruffly, and edged them forward. "Keep moving."

Emily was frightened too. Terrified, actually, but leaving Rufus and the carpetbag in the coach, she followed Jackson into the water. Her feet sank down into the sand, mud oozing between her toes. She had never in her life been this dirty. Never crossed a river holding her little boots over her head.

"Stay next to the raft, folks, because I know the lay of the land here. You don't want to be stepping too far to the right," the driver called from the front.

Emily tried to stay to the left, but every so often her foot went down into a hole and she teetered. Each time, however, she managed to get close to the raft again. Once, though, when she had moved away a little, she felt someone coming up from behind, squeezing between her and the raft. She was jostled out into deeper water and sank down as far as her chest. Holding her boots even higher, she tried to get back in line, but the person was coming on through, and Emily found herself even farther out into the river.

Now she was in water up to her neck. She started to

scream, to call out to Jackson, but she knew that once she said his name aloud, she would no longer be the silent brother who couldn't talk.

She looked up at the person who had so dangerously come between her and the raft, and the man with the silver-black hair only stared down at her with his weasel eyes and made no move to reach out and save her.

Luckily for Emily, Jackson glanced around at that moment to see how she was doing, and saw only the cap she'd been wearing afloat in the water.

"Eli!" he yelled, plunging after her.

It was Mr. Muffit, however, straggling along behind, who saw what had happened and managed to swim over to Emily. He pulled her, gasping and choking, back to safety, while Jackson rescued the cap.

"Thank you, mister," Jackson told the old man, whose beard was woefully wet.

"Eh, eh, eh," Mr. Muffit murmured, and sloshed on through the water.

Emily held on to the raft with one hand as she trudged forward, and Jackson came right behind. She was still coughing up water, and it dripped from her ears and eyelashes.

"Keep ahead of me from now on," Jackson told her, and didn't take his eyes off her the rest of the way across the river.

• • •

They finally reached the other side, but their travel got no easier. Now they entered the fearsome Deadman's Gulch that Oscar, Angus, and Jock had talked about. Once again they had to get out and walk, for the sand was so deep that the wheels of the stagecoach kept sinking.

By the time they could get back inside, Marigold had decided that she and her sister should get a turn sitting on the front bench, which was a bit less bumpy than the back and middle seats. So Oscar, Angus, and Jock took the middle seat, and the two grown sisters and Uncle Victor now faced backward.

Uncle Victor did not seem to appreciate this exchange at all, for he obviously preferred to see where he was going rather than to look at where he had been. But

Emily hated it even more, because now and then his eyes fell on her directly. Still, she was so exhausted from her close escape in the water that she rested her head on Jackson's shoulder and soon fell asleep.

She did not know how long she slept, but she woke with a jolt as the stagecoach came to a sudden stop.

"*Now* what?" Uncle Victor exclaimed.

Emily sat up and looked out.

A fallen tree blocked the way, and huge boulders on either side kept the horses from going forward. The driver called out for a few strong men to help move the tree.

But at that very moment, two bandits emerged on horseback around one of the rocks. One pointed his pistol at the driver, and the other opened the door of the coach. Marigold and Petunia screamed. Emily was frozen with fright.

When Uncle Victor tried to rise from his seat, the bandit placed his pistol against Victor's head and said quietly, "Nobody moves unless I tell him to."

So nobody moved, not even the man with the tiger

tattoo. Emily wondered if anyone in the coach was even breathing.

The bandit spoke again: "Now . . . easy-like . . . empty your pockets and open your bags. *All* of you." He started with Uncle Victor. When Emily's uncle hesitated, the bandit pressed the gun even harder to his head. "Give me all that's in your pockets," he said.

Uncle Victor had to obey. Out came a few silver coins and a couple of gold pieces. The bandit took it all. Uncle Victor looked as though he could chew the bandit in two, but not even he dared to move with a gun at his head.

When the bandit turned to the two sisters, however, Marigold fainted in Uncle Victor's lap, while Petunia reached over Marigold and clutched at his shirt.

"Save us! Save us!" she cried as Uncle Victor tried to pry her fingers loose.

The bandit started to laugh. "You got your hands full, mister," he said. "You want to get away, we got an extra horse out there." He took a ring off Marigold's finger as she opened her eyes, and she fainted all over again.

After he had taken Petunia's necklace and emptied the pockets of Oscar, Angus, and Jock, he took a few coins from the elderly man. Then he turned to Jackson and Emily.

There was nothing in Jackson's pockets but a piece of bread and a few crackers. When Emily opened her carpetbag for the bandit, she hoped he would not take out her dress and petticoat for all to see, and he didn't. He pointed to the little box with Rufus in it.

"Open it," he said, his gun still trained on the men.

No! No! Emily thought in terror. *Not Rufus!* She opened her mouth to protest, but Jackson elbowed her in the ribs.

"Open it, Eli," he said.

Emily lifted the lid of the box. The bandit saw the turtle and laughed. "Keep it, kid," he said. "Ain't got no use for a turtle."

But the horrible, awful truth was that Uncle Victor had seen Rufus too. Emily did not dare look at him but kept her eyes on her lap.

The bandit took all the gold and silver he had collected, the rings off the fingers of the ladies, and the watches from the pockets of the men, and stuffed it all in a sack, then backed out of the coach. He robbed the driver of both his money and his pistol as the second bandit trained his gun on them all. Finally, firing two shots in the air, they galloped off and were soon lost among the rocks and shrubs.

The men in the coach began to howl and growl, and the sisters sobbed and wailed. The driver came back to see that no one was hurt.

"We're all poorer than we were when we started, but we're alive," he said. "And I still need that tree removed from the road so we can continue the journey. Why don't you all get out and walk a little to calm yourselves."

So Oscar, Angus, and Jock moved the tree while the other passengers walked around to settle their nerves.

"I hope those bandits are caught and spend the rest of their lives in prison!" Marigold said.

"They ought to hang!" said Petunia. "I'd tie the noose myself."

Emily and Jackson walked over to the shade of a straggly tree, and stood staring at each other.

"That's about as scared as I've ever been," Jackson told her.

Emily had been frightened too, but she was not thinking about the bandits.

"He *saw*!" she said to Jackson, her voice trembling. "Uncle Victor saw Rufus!"

"Maybe he's forgotten Rufus," Jackson told her.

"He's thinking about that ten million dollars; that's what's on his mind." They turned as they saw the others getting into the coach again.

Something behind them moved. Uncle Victor grabbed Jackson by the back of the neck and Emily by the arm. And before either of them could speak, he looked down at Emily and said, "You fooled me once, Emily Wiggins, but you won't fool me again. There's not a soul in this carriage who will help you if I say you're my runaway niece. Either you come with me when we get to Redbud, or you won't get to Redbud at all. I'll deal with the boy later."

Now what in a devil's doughnut should Emily do?

TWELVE
Breaking Away

Trapped! As Emily crawled into the coach with Uncle Victor behind her, she felt as though the man with the tiger tattoo had chained the door after them. Jackson was shaking too as the stagecoach moved off again.

They crawled onto the backseat with Mr. Muffit as they had before, but Uncle Victor was on the first seat, facing backward, guarding the door. There were only a few more rest stops between here and Redbud, the driver had said. And now, instead of running into Aunt

Hilda's arms, Emily would have to go with Uncle Victor.

Strangely, her uncle did not announce to the others that Emily was his niece and had deceived everyone into believing that she was a boy who could not talk. Perhaps he felt that if he did, he would also have to explain to the others why she was hiding from him.

How Emily wished that Mrs. Ready, Mrs. Aim, and Mrs. Fire were here to advise her!

Mrs. Ready might say, "The problem is that many grown-ups think children should be seen and not heard."

And Mrs. Aim would say, "What if Emily tries to explain and no one believes her? Won't that just make things worse for her?"

And Mrs. Fire might say, "She musn't say a word. Even if they do believe her, Uncle Victor might promise them a share of the ten million dollars just to keep quiet about it."

So Emily was to remain Eli for the rest of the journey, but now that Uncle Victor knew who Eli really was, what would happen next?

Jackson was taking no chances. That night, all the

passengers stretched out on the sleeping platform while the stagecoach bounced along in the dark. Emily lay behind the elderly gentleman and Jackson lay behind her. As the others snored, Jackson whispered in her ear:

"Listen, Emily, we're got to have a plan. Your uncle could do away with you before we get to Redbud, just to get your fortune for himself. I heard the driver say we'll make the next change of horses about midnight. It's not a rest stop, so no one will be wakened to get off. You've got to climb out and hide. Leave everything but your turtle behind. I'll cover your carpetbag with my jacket, and they'll think we're both here asleep. Stay hidden long enough that the station man can't put you on a horse and catch up with the coach when he finds you."

Emily turned her head and stared wide-eyed into the darkness.

Jackson continued, "I'll ride on to Redbud and look for your aunt at the station. I'll give her your bag and tell her Victor's here too, trying to find you to get your money."

"But Uncle Victor will be mad at you when he finds I'm missing," Emily whispered back.

"Don't worry about me," said Jackson. "It's you he's after."

"But what will become of *me*? I'll be all alone!" Emily whispered, her voice faltering.

"You'll take a chance, Emily, that's what you'll do," whispered Jackson. "It'll be the bravest thing you ever did. Tell the men at the way station that you got off when the team was changed. Tell them you fell asleep and the coach went off without you. They'll put you on the next stagecoach coming through to Redbud. You'll just get to your aunt's a couple days later, that's all."

At that moment Mr. Muffit rolled over slowly until his whiskers were in Emily's face. His voice was so low that Emily could hardly hear him, but this time he didn't sound old at all:

"Listen to me," he whispered. "I am a secret stagecoach inspector. My job is to ride all the way to California to see how well the drivers do their job. No one must know who I am. Do as your friend says,

Emily. I'll help him make it appear that you are asleep here in the coach."

Emily and Jackson couldn't see the man's face in the darkness, but they lay openmouthed in surprise. His fake beard scratched Emily's forehead.

Emily wondered what the three neighbor women would suggest.

Mrs. Ready might say, "Emily must decide whether she can do the brave thing!"

Mrs. Aim would ask, "But should she trust the inspector?"

And perhaps Mrs. Fire would answer, "I'd trust him before I'd trust that snake of an uncle!"

Emily could hardly bear the thought of another delay in getting to Aunt Hilda's, but she whispered her thanks to the stagecoach inspector and turned to Jackson once again.

"You've been a good friend, and I wouldn't have made it this far without you. I hope you find a good family to live with in the West."

It was just as Jackson had said. The coach stopped around midnight only long enough to change horses.

Most of the passengers went on snoring, and fortunately, Uncle Victor was one of them. As it was still dark and the stationmaster was busy with the animals, no one noticed the small child being helped out the window by a man with a beard. Emily dropped silently to the ground and ran around a corner of the way station.

A few minutes later the driver cracked his whip and the stagecoach was off again, each bend in the road taking Jackson farther and farther away.

Emily had never felt so alone—*really* alone. She crept back to the stable where the horses and mules were kept and dug a little nest for herself in the hay. She was still in Jackson's britches, still in Jackson's shirt. Her socks were filthy, her little boots were muddy, and her hair stuck out in short brown spikes all over her head. Meanwhile, her dress and petticoat and bonnet were on their way to Aunt Hilda's.

She opened Rufus's box and kissed his little face. His skin and shell looked dry. "Oh, please stay alive, Rufus!" she told him. "You're all I have from my mother." As soon as it was light, she would find some water for him to drink, some bugs for him to eat, and some grass that he might crawl through.

She wished she could explain to him that it would be only two more days before another stagecoach arrived to take her to Aunt Hilda's, but she kissed him instead, and he tucked his head back under his shell. Emily fell asleep.

• • •

Something cold and metallic touched the side of Emily's leg, and she jumped and opened her eyes.

A man's voice said, "Where the dickens did *you* come from?" He was standing there with a pitchfork, feeding the mules and staring wide-eyed at Emily. "Horace!" he called. "Come see what we got here!"

A second man, carrying a bucket of oats, came around the corner of the stall. "How'd you get here, boy?" the first man asked. "You come in with that stagecoach a few hours ago?"

"I guess so," said Emily, and it seemed strange to be talking out loud. Her voice sounded strange even to her. "I must have missed it when it took off again, and crawled back here to sleep."

"Where you headed?" asked the man named Horace.

"I'm going to live with my aunt Hilda in Redbud," Emily said.

"She's expecting you?" the man asked.

"She says she'll expect me when she sees me, and she'll be meeting each stagecoach as it comes in till I get there," Emily answered.

"Well, looks like you'll be here at Parsnip Pass till day after tomorrow," the first man said. "But don't think you're going to hang around here gettin' into mischief. You want to eat, you got to work. What's your name?"

"Eli," Emily told him.

"Then come along, Eli, and I'll show you how to muck the stable."

For the next few hours, Emily fed the horses and forked out the muck from the floor of the stable. She pulled up buckets of water from the well, brushed the horses, rinsed the tin plates after dinner, washed the men's socks, soaked beans, and generally made herself useful.

Her arms were stronger than when she'd first left home. Her legs were steadier, her back was straighter, and she had a good appetite at mealtime. The way-station men let her put Rufus in a little pen outside the door, where he had fresh water, fresh grass to crawl through, and whatever bugs he could catch.

When another coach to Redbud arrived two days later, the way-station men were sorry to see her go.

"Good luck to you, Eli," they told Emily as she climbed aboard with Rufus in his little box.

The driver of the stage wasn't especially glad to have her, as there were six Chinese workers on board already, heading west to build a railroad; he did not know how well a small boy would get along with them.

But Emily was used to being quiet, being alone, and being polite. The six workers spoke to each other in Chinese and ignored her, so Emily played with Rufus and tried to imagine how shocked everyone in the stagecoach must have been—Uncle Victor in particular—when they'd discovered she was missing. Because she had slipped out in the middle of the night, it would have been hours later and several way stations farther before anyone had realized she was gone. Jackson was so good at lying, she was sure he had made up a good story, and Mr. Muffit, who was really an inspector, would have backed him up.

All afternoon they rode, and after the next stop, where Emily got off and stretched, she curled up on the backseat. She knew that by the following morning, she would be in Redbud. This was such a happy thought that she began to doze at once, Rufus's box clutched in her hand, and finally fell asleep to the rocking of the stagecoach and the snoring of the Chinese workers.

The next way station was not a place for passengers to get off—just to change horses—and Emily opened her eyes only long enough to see a fresh team being led out from the stable as the station men with their lanterns led the other team back to the barn.

But suddenly, before the stagecoach started off again, it dipped and swayed. Someone sat down on the seat next to her, and a low voice said, "You've come to the end of the line, Emily Wiggins." The man with the tiger tattoo had a tight hold on her arm.

Was this really the beatin' cheatin' end of the line for Emily?

THIRTEEN

Going Home

Emily stared in dismay at her uncle. How could this be?

While the Chinese workers sat dozing, Uncle Victor continued in his growly voice, "The next stop is Redbud. If that aunt of yours is there waiting for you, you'll tell her you've decided to live with me. We'll go to the nearest courthouse or whatever they've got, and we'll sign a paper saying that you're Emily Wiggins, daughter of Constance Wiggins, my sister, and I'm your legal guardian." He gave her arm a little twist.

"And from now on, you scheming, sniveling good-for-nothing, you'll do as I say."

A week ago, perhaps, Emily Wiggins would have cowered before her uncle, too frightened to speak. But the long sleep in the stagecoach had refreshed her, the work at the way station had given her confidence, and the food had given her strength.

Emily stared into the eyes of the man with the tiger tattoo and said, "I won't."

A look of surprise flashed over Uncle Victor's face, and then he growled, with a cruel smile, "You will!"

It was then that Emily realized he was holding Rufus's box. *Thumpa thumpa thumpa*—her heart almost stopped. She reached out to grab the box, but Victor only narrowed his eyes and held it out of reach.

"When we get off this coach, Emily Wiggins, you will tell your aunt goodbye. And if you don't . . ." He held the box up even higher, and Emily could hear the *scritch, scratch* of Rufus's little claws on the sides as Victor tipped it back and forth. "If you don't," he continued, "if you give one hint to your aunt that you don't want to go with me, I will squash your turtle flatter than an old piece of shoe leather. I will crack his head to pieces like a walnut. I will throw him in a pig trough for the hogs to eat, and I will make you sorry you were ever born."

Emily felt weak. How could this have happened? Jackson had planned her escape so carefully, and now . . . ! For one brief moment, she *almost* wondered if Jackson had told her uncle where she was. But then Uncle Victor went on:

"You and that boy thought you could trick me, huh? Thought I'd go all the way to Redbud thinkin' you were asleep under that old man's jacket? When I finally figured out you'd stayed behind, I got off at a station to wait for the next coach to Redbud, 'cause I knew you'd be on it." His eyes narrowed. "And every day a coach passed us going back to Callaway, a coach we could've been on, I got madder and meaner. If there's any more trouble, first it'll be your turtle that goes, and then it'll be you."

Emily's eyes flashed in return. "Even if I tell Aunt

Hilda I want to go with you, she'll know! She *knows* I don't want to live with you, and she'll *make* you let me go!"

Her uncle laughed, a rumbling laugh from deep inside his chest, and his gold tooth gleamed. "I'll bet I'm twice as big and twice as strong as that aunt of yours, and there isn't a judge alive who'll believe you rather than me, your next of kin. Even the Child Catchers know that!"

One of the Chinese workers opened his eyes and watched for a moment, then closed them again. But Emily's eyes filled with tears. How could she have believed that Jackson, her friend, could plan something like this? The man with the tiger tattoo didn't need any help being mean. There was enough meanness inside him to fill a bathtub, Emily thought. Her tears only made him laugh, and every so often he would tip Rufus's box and make him go skidding from one side to the other. Some of the Chinese workers watched and listened sleepily, then drifted off again.

As the sky began to lighten, Emily pressed her face against the carriage window to stop the tears. She had thought perhaps she would see signs of Redbud before they got there, but all she saw were scrub pines and sand and a coyote or two.

Uncle Victor stared out the window over Emily's shoulder. "If this isn't the saddest, meanest, driest, hottest country I ever did see," he said. "I'd get out right now if there was a living soul to put us up."

I could be happy anywhere with Aunt Hilda, Emily thought, *but I wouldn't be happy even in a* palace *with you!*

At long last Emily saw some fence posts, and farther on, some cattle. A cottage . . . some sheep . . . some trees . . . a barn . . . and finally the driver blew his bugle to announce to the little settlement of Redbud that the coach to the West was coming in. The Chinese workers roused themselves and stretched.

"Now, *remember,*" Uncle Victor said, grabbing Emily's arm so hard that it hurt. "You tell your aunt you're coming with me. And if you don't . . ." He shook Rufus's box so hard that it rattled, and Emily felt her anger growing bigger and bigger inside her chest like a balloon.

The Chinese workers began to talk among themselves. This was a way station where they could get a bite to eat before the coach went on. Emily thought how often she had imagined this moment—had imagined how happy and excited she would be when the stagecoach pulled up and her aunt was there to meet her. How happy to have a place where she belonged. Where she was loved.

There was another blast from the bugle, but this time it was to hurry along a large flock of sheep crossing the road some distance from the station. But the sheep would not be hurried, and the stagecoach had to stop.

"It'll be a few more minutes, folks," the driver called down. "We've got to wait for these sheep. You can get out and stretch a bit if you like."

One of the Chinese workers opened the door and got out.

"It's okay, driver," Uncle Victor called back. "My nephew and I will get off here. He's excited to be with me again."

He climbed out, pulling Emily after him.

"Liar, liar, pants on fire," Emily muttered angrily.

"No more liar than you are, dressing up like a boy," Uncle Victor muttered back.

Far down the road, Emily could see a small group of people standing in front of the way station. She was quite sure that the woman in the group, in a blue-checked dress, was Aunt Hilda. And there, standing right beside her, was . . . *Jackson!*

What would the neighbor women tell her to do if they were here? Emily wondered.

"She surely would not want Rufus to be hurt," Mrs. Ready might say.

"But what can she possibly do?" Mrs. Aim would ask.

And Mrs. Fire would answer, "Give it a go, Emily. Go!"

Uncle Victor had one hand on the back of Emily's neck, and in his other hand he held the box with Rufus in it.

He pushed her roughly forward, and at that very moment the Chinese worker stuck out his foot. Down Uncle Victor went.

"Good day!" the man said, smiling at Emily.

Instantly she stepped hard on Uncle Victor's wrist,

forcing his fingers to let go of the box. “Ow!” he bellowed.

Quick as a flash, Emily snatched up Rufus's box, and rising to her feet, one bootlace flapping, she ran. On she raced, faster than she had ever run, through the baaing sheep, with Uncle Victor behind her. She ran so fast that the wind whistled in her ears.

“Aunt Hilda!” she bellowed, in the greatest, loudest voice she had ever known, sending the sheep scattering in all directions. A few seconds later she threw herself into her aunt's arms.

But Uncle Victor was right at her heels. “You miserable little wretch!” he exclaimed, panting, his clothes askew. He turned to Emily's aunt. “Well, Hilda,” he growled, looking at the three men who had come to the way station with her. “I see you've brought a few farm boys to welcome me to Redbud. I'm here to tell you that the girl's coming to live with me, and if you fight me on this, I'll take you to court.”

Thumpa thumpa thumpa, went Emily's heart, and she clung to the round woman even harder. In the horse-drawn wagon behind her aunt, a black dog with a red kerchief around its neck wagged its tail and showed its pink tongue.

"Hello, Victor," said Aunt Hilda. "Jackson here told me exactly what you are up to, and I'd like you to meet my three closest neighbors out where I live."

Emily looked around. One of the men was carrying an ax. Another was carrying a pitchfork. And the third man was holding a shotgun.

"How do you do?" said the man with the ax. "I live just up the road from Hilda, and I'm a lawyer."

"I live *down* the road from Hilda, and I'm the judge in these parts," said the man with the pitchfork.

The third man held on to his shotgun. "I live over by the river, and I happen to be the sheriff," he said. "We'd welcome you to Redbud, mister, but I'd suggest you buy yourself a ticket for the first stagecoach heading back to where you came from."

"And Emily stays here," said the judge. "That *is* Emily, isn't it?"

Aunt Hilda held Emily out in front of her and looked her over, smiling.

"It's Emily, all right," said Jackson, grinning.

"I'm pretty dirty," Emily said, embarrassed.

"It'll wash," said Aunt Hilda.

"We cut my hair," said Emily.

"It'll grow," said her aunt.

"My turtle needs some grass and something to eat," said Emily, opening the box and letting Rufus have some air. "And I'm pretty hungry myself."

"Honey," said her aunt, "I got us a mess of beans on the stove, some bread on the table, and a pie on the shelf. I'll fix you up in no time. And I've told Jackson he doesn't need to go any farther. He's going to make his home right here with us."

"Hooray!" shouted Emily, throwing her arms around Jackson and giving him a hug. Jackson's smile was as wide as a dinner plate.

Uncle Victor had slunk off to the way station, but now he was coming back.

"Hey!" he yelled. "They say there's no place for me to sleep in there. This lousy town have a hotel where a man can lie down?"

The three neighbor men laughed.

"Why, we're just country boys here in Redbud, mister. No hotel to put you up, and if there was, they wouldn't take the likes of you," said the sheriff. "Might be we could find you a bunk in the jailhouse. Or maybe a pigpen you could use. Course, the next station's Crow Point, if you want to walk."

There was a sudden commotion down the street as a group of women approached, each holding a parasol.

"*There* he is!" cried a familiar voice. "Oh, Vic-tor! We've been looking for you!"

"Oh, Tiger Man! Remember us?" called another. And turning to her friends, Petunia cooed, "I *told* you he was on his way to Redbud, the man with the tiger tattoo!"

"And the handsome curling mustache!" said Marigold.

As the women rushed forward, Uncle Victor took off for Crow Point, and the last anyone ever saw of him, he was running to beat the band.

The sheriff chuckled. "He's got himself a twenty-mile hike."

Aunt Hilda reached down and gave Emily the longest, tightest hug she'd ever had.

"And I've got me about twenty acres for you and Jackson to explore to your hearts' content, with plenty of grass for your turtle," she said. "Let's go home."

And dooby dabby, don't you know, that's exactly what they did.

About the Author

PHYLLIS REYNOLDS NAYLOR says she was never as quiet as Emily Wiggins, but she never had such excitement, either. And she is extremely glad that she never had a relative like Uncle Victor. It was great fun figuring out what would happen to Emily next, as long as Phyllis herself didn't have to go through it.

Phyllis Naylor tries never to write the same type of book twice in a row. Many readers know her best through *Shiloh,* winner of the Newbery Award, but others have followed her boy/girl battle series, beginning with *The Boys Start the War* and *The Girls Get Even.* Her most recent book, about a girl in Kentucky coal country, was *Faith, Hope, and Ivy June*.

Mrs. Naylor lives in Gaithersburg, Maryland, with her husband, Rex. They have two grown sons and four grandchildren: Sophia, Tressa, Garrett, and Beckett. Naylor is the author of more than 135 books. When she is not writing, she enjoys attending the theater, swimming, and doing almost anything with her family.